Filthy Appeal

RAMONA GRAY

Adult Reading Material

Cover design by The Final Wrap

ISBN-13: 978-1-988826-55-4

Chapter One

"I'm worried about you, Libby." My mother's voice was cutting in and out, and I shifted my cell phone to my other ear. I crossed the room and drew back the drapes, staring down at the park across from me. Dusk was falling. There was a glow of green and red Christmas lights that were strung through the trees in the park, illuminating the people hurrying down the shovelled paths.

"I told you, the roads were fine. I'm at the hotel and I pick up the key for my new place tomorrow afternoon. I'm good."

"You're not good. How can you be?" My mother almost wailed into the phone.

I tried to hold in my sigh of irritation. "Because I've just landed my dream job? I'm not only the first female partner at the law firm of Martin, Clarke and Bones, I'm the youngest partner in the history of the firm, Mom."

"What good is a dream job when your heart is broken?"

"My heart is not broken."

"I know you still love him."

"No, I don't," I snapped. "He cheated on me. Repeatedly. In our bed with a twenty-two-year-old."

"Honey," my mother said, "I know that Wayne made a terrible decision and I understand how difficult it's been for you, but men have needs."

"Don't, Mom. It's been a long day and I'm tired," I warned.

"Hear me out, honey. You were working a lot of overtime and you had - "

"I was working to secure our future," I hissed into the phone. "Do you think Wayne was going to provide for us by being a short-order cook at a second-rate diner?"

"See, that's what I'm talking about," my mother said.

"I have no idea what you mean," I said.

"You were always belittling him, honey. I've had some long talks with Wayne since you broke up with him and he told me how you didn't approve of his job or his dream of one day owning his own restaurant. If you want to keep a man, you have to be supportive of their dreams. Add in the fact that you've let yourself go in the last few years and is it any wonder that Wayne was tempted to stray?"

I wished I could say I was shocked by my mother's behaviour, but I wasn't. I'd spent my entire life listening to her lecture me on all the ways I failed at – well – everything. I'd already heard this particular gem of a lecture twice before, but I suddenly couldn't stand to listen to it for a moment longer. Unfortunately, my mother was relentless.

"You did so well to lose all that weight, honey, and it's a real shame that you lost focus and gained it back."

"I didn't lose focus. I was very busy at work and I got tired of starving myself and going to the gym every night for two hours," I said. "Just because I'm fat and busy at work doesn't give Wayne the right to cheat on me, Mom."

"Of course it doesn't," my mother said. "But, honey, you know men are visual creatures. They want to be proud of their lady and you can't blame Wayne for not being proud of the fact that you've gained forty pounds in the last two years. You have such a pretty face, Libby, it's a shame that - "

"I have to go," I interrupted.

"Honey, wait! We haven't talked about Christmas. What day are you driving back?"

"We did talk about Christmas, remember? I said I wasn't going to be there."

"I didn't think you meant it," my mother said. "You're really going to leave me all alone on Christmas?"

"You won't be alone," I said. "You're going to grandma and grandpa's and the rest of your siblings will be there as well."

She carried on like she hadn't heard a word I'd said. Honestly, she probably hadn't.

"Christmas is for family, Elizabeth. Family!"

"It's a very busy time at the firm, and they needed me to start this week," I lied.

My mother sighed dramatically. "Well, my only child is abandoning me for her career. I guess I can understand where Wayne is coming from."

Anger and frustration and a healthy dose of hurt settled in my stomach and I blinked back the tears savagely. "That's not what I'm doing and you know it. I have to go. Good night, Mom. I'll call you in a few days when I'm settled."

I pushed the end button on my phone before she could reply and could barely restrain myself from throwing my phone across the room. I leaned my forehead against the window, closed my eyes, and tried not to let my mother's obvious disappointment in me change my mind about what I was going to do.

I straightened and crossed the hotel room to study myself in the full-length mirror. I was wearing my tightest pair of jeans and a shimmery blue top that hugged my breasts and had a scandalously low neckline. My push-up bra was doing a marvelous job of keeping my tits where they were supposed to be, and I studied my cleavage before pulling self-consciously at my top. I was certain that if I took too deep of a breath, my boobs would fall right out of my shirt. I glanced at my suitcase and briefly considered changing my shirt before turning to the mirror again. I needed a pep talk stat.

"Elizabeth Gertrude Brecken, you are not changing your shirt. One does not simply walk into a generic hotel bar and seduce a stranger wearing a t-shirt. Your tits are amazing and you're going to need them out front and center and working overtime."

I turned and stared at my butt. I couldn't hide the size of my ass or thickness of my thighs or my extra-large muffin top. Not in these clothes. For a moment, I mourned the loss of my thinness before I shook my head. I was being stupid. Until I walked in on Wayne banging the twenty-two-year-old like a screen door in a tornado, I'd been perfectly content with my larger body.

Always a chubby kid and teenager, I'd finally grown tired of my mother's constant nagging about my weight and started a strict regime of diet and exercise when I entered university. I'd stayed thin through starvation and exercise until the last two years. My busy career and my lack of enthusiasm for constantly monitoring what I ate, led to a slow but gradual weight gain. I still exercised on a regular basis and I ate healthy for the most part, but my body wasn't meant to be thin. I wasn't bothered by it, it was a relief to finally be myself again, and Wayne hadn't seemed upset by it either. Of course, the twenty-two-year-old he was screwing had the lithe body of a gymnast and when I'd confronted him, he had said that -

I cut off that thought immediately. Bile rose in my throat and I swallowed it down. Best not to think about Wayne and his betrayal. Despite what my mother thought, I was supportive of his dream of owning his own restaurant. It wasn't my fault that he lacked the motivation to actually pursue his dream.

I shook off the memories of Wayne and grabbed my purse from the bed. I was starting a new job in a new city and I couldn't be happier. Christmas was a week away and yes, I would be spending it alone for the first time in my life, but even that didn't upset me. My new company was more than willing to let me start in the new year. They were a little surprised that I wanted to start so close to the holidays, but I couldn't get away from my old life fast enough. Given the choice between spending Christmas alone binge watching my favourite shows on Netflix, or spending Christmas with my mother listening to her lecture me on all my shortcomings, it wasn't hard to choose.

"Netflix," I said to my reflection in the mirror. "Definitely Netflix. Okay, girl, let's do this."

Libby, are you sure you want to do this?

I ignored my inner me. My self-esteem had taken a nosedive when I walked in on Wayne and his floozy. While I might have been happy with how my career was going, there was a stupid part of me that was desperate to find out if I could still seduce a guy into sleeping with me. It had been years since I dated, and while I wasn't interested in dating right now, I was interested in finding a man to fuck. I blushed at my dirty thoughts, but if I couldn't be truthful with myself about what I wanted, then I shouldn't be going to the damn hotel bar in the first place.

Wayne and I hadn't had sex in months, I was single, and I was in a city where no one knew me. I wanted to prove to myself that I was still attractive enough to land a man, even with a muffin top and oversize ass.

Prove it to yourself or to your mother? Inner me whispered. *We both know you're not a one-night stand kind of woman. Also, men like thin girls, not a fatty like you.*

I spun around abruptly and stalked out of the room, letting the door slam behind me. I was getting laid tonight, no matter what.

„ ‟

For a Saturday night, the hotel bar was relatively empty and my prospects for having sex with a stranger seemed dismally slim. Although, it was still early, I told myself. In this particular case, maybe the early bird didn't get the worm.

Girl, you need to look for something bigger than a worm. You've spent years denying it, but Wayne's dick was small and nothing special. You need a man with a big dick who knows how to use it.

When had I become such a damn nymphomaniac? I had always liked sex, but in the last month or so I'd become obsessed with it. Become obsessed with finding someone who would find me attractive and sexy at my current size. Someone who wouldn't tell me that –

Nope, I wasn't going there. Reliving the memory of Wayne telling me that my weight was crushing him – both figuratively and literally – was a terrible idea. I straightened my back before sweeping my gaze over the bar. There was a group of businessmen sitting at a table close to the entrance. They were talking loudly, and from the look of their flailing hands and red faces, they'd already had too much to drink. I crossed all of them off my mental "try and have sex with" list.

A few couples were sitting at the booths and tables scattered around the bar. A trio of women wearing jeans and t-shirts – they had the harried look of overworked mothers – were conversing quietly. The one closest to me glanced at the street entrance and I followed her gaze when her eyes widened and she nudged her friend sitting next to her.

My breath caught in my throat. The two gods who had just walked in were smiling at the hostess and even from here she looked flustered and nervous. I couldn't blame her. Both men were well over six feet tall with broad shoulders and narrow hips. The one on the left had dark hair, and he was slightly taller and heavier than his friend. I could see the muscles bulging in his arms as he stuck his hands into the back pockets of his faded jeans. The motion made his t-shirt cling to his abdomen and my pussy made a weird little flutter as I stared at the ridges of muscles. His friend had a leaner build and sandy-brown coloured hair and I took a deep shuddering breath when he grinned at the hostess and two deep dimples appeared in his cheeks.

Oh God, my panties were getting wet. The two men practically screamed sex and for one moment I allowed myself the fantasy of sleeping with one of them.

One of them? You want to choose? Go for both!

I almost laughed out loud. I was barely the type of girl who had a one-night stand with one man, let alone two. Besides, men who looked like them were not interested in women who looked like me.

Of course, that didn't prevent my heart from stopping and then galloping back into beat when the dark-haired god glanced my way. I stood frozen to the spot as his gaze drifted down my body before returning to my face. Was that... lust on his face?

I could feel my cheeks burning and I sucked in my gut and looked away. I was an idiot. The denim-wearing god and his dimpled friend were way, *way* out of my league. I was wasting my time even fantasizing about them.

Forcing myself not to peek at them again, I studied the curved wooden bar. Mirrors lined the wall behind it and I studied the reflection of the lone man sitting at the bar. He had olive coloured skin and black hair that was thinning on top. He looked a little older than me and he was clean shaven and wearing a custom-made suit. He was handsome enough and he looked...safe. Like someone I could seduce.

Keeping my head high, I walked to the bar and slid onto the stool beside him. He glanced at my face and his gaze dipped briefly to my cleavage before he returned to staring at his glass of wine. Not exactly an encouraging start but I checked for a wedding band anyway. His ring finger was bare. It was time to put my plan – code name "bang a total stranger" – into motion.

I waved at the bartender. She took her sweet time walking over and gave me a polite smile. I ordered a glass of wine and when she returned with it, I fumbled my money out of my wallet. God, I was so nervous.

I took a few sips of wine for courage before clearing my throat. "Hi there. My name is Libby. What's yours?"

The man glanced at me again. "Dwayne."

I jerked wildly and nearly fell off the stool. Fuck, that was too close to Wayne for comfort. The man arched his eyebrow at me and I gave him a weak smile. "Sorry, I'm a little clumsy."

"Sure," he replied.

I held out my hand and after a moment, he shook it briefly. His hand was soft and sweaty and his nails were perfectly manicured. He tapped one finger against his wine glass as I said, "So, are you in town for business?"

He nodded but didn't offer any more information. I took another sip of wine. "What do you do?"

"Marketing," he said.

I waited for him to ask what I did and when he didn't, said, "Do you enjoy it?"

"Yes." He drank some wine and I was encouraged when he took a quick peek at my tits. Maybe he was shy.

"That's good. Enjoying your work is important. I'm a…"

The dark-haired god sat down on the stool on my other side. His dimpled friend had already sat down next to him. The butterflies flickered to life in my stomach and I forgot about Dwayne from marketing as I inhaled. The dark-haired man smelled incredible and I gripped my wine glass as the bartender came hurrying over.

"Hi there. What can I get you guys?" She placed her hands on the edge of the bar and bent a little at the waist, giving them both a smile and a good look down her shirt. She had nothing on me when it came to tits, but I supposed that didn't matter. She was beautiful with tanned skin and long dark hair and a slender body. She probably did yoga every day and drank organic kale smoothies. Seeing as she was the most gorgeous woman in the bar, there was no doubt in my mind that she'd be going home with one of the gods tonight.

So, wait to see which one she takes and then you take the other!

I almost scoffed out loud as they ordered beers and the bartender gave them a slow inviting smile before hurrying off to get their drinks. Just because they happened to sit next to me at the bar didn't mean I could seduce which ever one the bartender rejected. No, they weren't for me. I needed to concentrate on nice, safe Dwayne. He was probably amazing in bed. Didn't they say that the men who looked stuffy and stiff were actually animals in the sack?

Yes, I decided as the bartender returned with the beers, that's what they said. Dwayne was probably incredible in bed and, dammit, I was determined to find out for certain. I ignored the god sitting on my left side and turned back to Dwayne.

"So, Dwayne, what do you like to do for fun?"

Dwayne smiled condescendingly at me before saying, "Look, Lily, you seem like a nice lady but I'm not interested in you. I like my women a little more fit, okay?"

Hot shame flooded my cheeks as Dwayne drank the last of his wine, slid off the stool and walked away without looking back. I clenched my hand around my wine glass as I blinked back the hot tears. No doubt the hottie sitting next to me had heard every word. I was beyond humiliated. Why the fuck had I ever thought a man would find me attractive? Wayne and my mother were right. Men didn't want a fat girl, they wanted –

"You're going to break that glass, sweetheart." A big hand, warm and covered in hard calluses wrapped around mine. He tugged lightly on my fingers. "Let go of the glass."

I let go and dropped my hand into my lap. It latched onto my other one and they worried and twisted together as I stared dully at the top of the bar. Oh God, I couldn't stand the humiliation.

"You okay?" His voice was a deep rasp that sent shivers down my spine.

I nodded and croaked, "I have to go."

"He's an idiot, sweetheart."

Now the tears were slipping down my cheeks and I brushed them away. "Th-thanks. I have to go now."

"Don't go, love." A second voice, just as low as the first, spoke from my right. The dimpled god had moved to sit on Dwayne's empty stool and I groaned inwardly as he said, "Have a drink with us."

"I shouldn't," I whispered.

"You should," the dark-haired one said. He signalled for the bartender and ordered me another glass of wine. When it arrived, he paid for it and handed it over. I took two large swallows and was about to take a third when the glass was tugged from my hand.

"Whoa, slow down, love," the dimpled god said.

"We don't want you getting drunk on us."

I didn't reply. I couldn't look either of them in the eye, and fresh embarrassment washed over me when the dark-haired one said, "He really is an idiot. You shouldn't listen to a word he says, Lily."

"Libby," I whispered. "My name is Libby. He-he got it wrong."

"See? Complete idiot," the dark-haired man said. "My name is Seth and this is my friend Theo."

"It's a pleasure to meet you, Libby." Theo held out his hand and after a moment I shook it. His hand had rough calluses as well that scraped across my palm. "Are you visiting our city for pleasure or business?"

"I – I just moved here. I'm staying at the hotel tonight because my, uh, place isn't ready until tomorrow."

"Welcome to Mansford," Seth said. "I assure you that not all the men here are assholes like old Dwayne."

I shrugged and Seth leaned closer. I shivered when I felt his warm breath on the side of my face. "He's wrong, Libby. You look - "

"I know what I look like," I interrupted. "Thank you for the glass of wine but I'm dying of embarrassment and I want to forget this ever happened."

I grabbed my purse but before I slid off the stool, Seth said, "Libby, wait."

The command in his voice kept me frozen to the stool. I didn't object when he tugged my purse from my hand and placed it back on the bar before taking my hand and rubbing his thumb over my palm.

I was trembling and my skin felt hot and tight. I watched Seth's thumb rub across my palm and shamefully made a soft moan when he leaned in and brushed his lips against my cheek.

"You're beautiful, Libby and much too good for a man like him."

"I'm not," I whispered.

"You are," he insisted. "Look at me."

I dragged my gaze away from his thumb and stared into his eyes. They were the colour of dark chocolate and a shiver went down my spine when he dipped his head and pressed a feather-light kiss against my mouth.

I whimpered quietly, my body arching toward him and a ghost of a smile crossed his lips. "Beautiful and responsive. Your turn, Theo."

I blinked at him but before I could ask him what he meant, Theo was cupping the back of my neck and tugging gently on it. I turned to face him and moaned when his mouth descended on mine. The tip of his tongue traced my lower lip and I parted my lips immediately. He pulled back and smiled at me, squeezing the back of my neck before dropping his hand from my neck and picking up his beer.

He took a long drink as I said in a low and shaky voice, "What is happening?"

"Why are you in this bar tonight, Libby?" Seth's voice was right in my ear and I licked my lips as both men crowded close. The babbled conversation of the other patrons in the bar faded away and I had to work very hard not to lean against the warm bodies of either men. Their shoulders brushed mine and their heads were tilted toward me.

"I came here because I," my face flushed, "I couldn't sleep and I thought a nightcap might help."

Seth's eyebrow arched up and he glanced at Theo. "Do you believe her, Theo?"

"No," Theo said with a small grin. "Do you?"

Seth shook his head and I gasped when his big hand rested on my thigh. His fingers pushed between them and he rubbed my inner thigh as Theo put his hand on my lower back and traced tiny circles.

"I think you're lying to us, sweetheart," Seth said.

"I'm not," I whispered.

"Lying gets you a spanking," Theo said.

All the muscles in my pussy clenched in a heart-stopping spasm of pleasure and my nipples beaded into hard points. I was nearly panting now and a flush was rising up my neck. Why did the thought of being spanked by them bring a shameful amount of liquid to my pussy? Spanking wasn't my kink.

How do you know? Old stick-in-the-mud Wayne liked two positions and wouldn't know a kink if it smacked him in the face.

"Tell us why you're really here, Libby," Seth said.

His big hand squeezed my thigh and the words came tumbling out of me in a low rush. "I came home one day and my boyfriend was having sex with a much younger and thinner woman in our bed. When I asked him why he said, he-he said ..."

I trailed off and swallowed past the aching burn in my throat. I couldn't say it. It was too humiliating. Seth rubbed my thigh and Theo pressed a gentle kiss against my cheek.

"How are you guys doing? Need a fresh drink?"

The bartender was back and I stared grimly at my hands in my lap as Seth said, "No thank you."

"Are you sure?" The bartender was persistent, I'd give her that. "I can bring you a menu if you're hungry."

"No thank you," Seth repeated. "We want privacy please."

"Oh, of course." The bartender sounded both surprised and deflated and my inner voice cheered loudly. Score one for the big girl.

When she was gone, Seth said, "Tell us, Libby."

I hesitated and then said, "If I don't, will you spank me?"

What the fuck?

"Yes," Theo said in a low voice. "We'll bend you over the bed, pull down your jeans and your panties and spank your lovely ass until it's covered in our handprints."

I moaned, and Seth squeezed my thigh again before grinning at Theo. "I think we might have better luck if we threaten *not* to spank her."

"Oh God," I whispered. "What is wrong with me?"

"Nothing," Theo said. "Tell us what we want to know, love."

"He cheated on me because I'd gained weight."

I didn't have to tell them exactly what he said.

I'd just make sure that if I did have sex with one of them, I wouldn't be on top. Easy.

I jerked when Seth made a low curse. Theo was studying me and I closed my eyes and said, "I came to the bar because I wanted to find someone to sleep with me. I wanted to convince myself that I was still attractive and desirable. I just wanted a fling, you know?"

"Why did you choose Dwayne?" Seth asked.

"Well, because he looked safe and," I paused, "attainable for someone who looked like me."

"You saw us when we first came in, didn't you?" Seth said.

I nodded and he squeezed my leg again. "You saw the way I looked at you. You knew I wanted you."

"I didn't," I lied.

"You did," he insisted.

"I – I didn't think it was real," I whispered.

His hand moved off my thigh and he turned me on the stool to face him before kissing me again. This time there was no gentleness in the kiss. He took my mouth with a hard possessiveness that made me ache with need. His tongue pushed past my lips and flicked against mine. I forgot that we were in the bar and returned his kiss with an eagerness that surprised me. My heart was pounding in my ears and I was pressing myself against the stool in a vain attempt to ease the ache between my thighs. When Seth pulled away, I nearly fell off the stool. Only Theo's hand on my hip kept me in my seat.

"I want you, little Libby," Seth said bluntly. "I

want to take you back to your hotel room, spread your legs and fuck you into the best orgasm of your life. Does that clear things up for you?"

I stared mutely at him before whispering, "You – you're not safe."

He grinned. "Is safe what you really want, sweetheart?"

"I don't know."

Theo's breath was warm on the back of my neck. "It isn't, love."

I had forgotten completely about Theo and I shivered when he pressed up against my back and kissed my neck. "Play with us tonight, Libby. I promise it'll be a night you won't forget."

"Us?" I whispered. I gave Seth a shocked look and he nodded gravely.

"We're a package deal, sweetheart."

"I – I can't take both of you to my room," I said in a low voice.

"Why not?" Seth asked.

"Well, because it isn't – I mean, what would people say if they knew that I…"

I trailed off and Seth grinned at me. "We won't say anything if you won't."

I didn't reply and Theo kissed the side of my neck again. "Say yes, love. We want you very much. You want a one-night stand, let us give it to you."

"You can't tell anyone I did this," I whispered. I was being ridiculous. Seth and Theo's rough hands and the way they were dressed suggested they were laborers. The thin layer of sawdust that clung to Seth's jeans and the paint spatters on Theo's shirt meant they most likely worked in a trade. This was a large city and since my circle of friends would probably be the people I worked with, we wouldn't be in the same social circle. After tonight, I'd never see them again.

Then take them to your room and fuck them! For God's sake, you could have the time of your life tonight if you'd stop thinking about what others might say.

Inner me was right. I came to the bar looking to find a man who found me attractive and wanted to fuck me. I had found not one, but two, and suddenly I was getting cold feet? Fuck that. No, not fuck that – fuck *them*, both of them… a lot.

"We won't say a word, love," Theo said. "Cross our hearts, hope to die."

Seth made an X across his chest before winking at me.

"Yes," I said abruptly.

Chapter Two

Neither of them waited for me to say anything else. Theo urged me off the stool and Seth took my hand in a firm grip. We left the bar and although I was certain that everyone was staring at us, in reality no one gave us a second look. We rode up the elevator in complete silence. The men flanked me, Seth still holding my hand and Theo resting his on the small of my back.

At the door to my room, Seth took the card key from me and opened the door before handing it back. I tucked it into my purse as they followed me into my room.

"Nice room," Seth said as Theo crossed the room and drew the curtains shut.

"Thank you," I said. My voice was an anxious squeak and my entire body was shaking as Seth drew me into his arms.

"Don't be nervous, little Libby."

"I've never slept with two men before," I said. "So, how does this work? Are you two, um, fond of each other as well?"

Seth shook his head. "No, Theo and I are only into women."

"Okay," I whispered. "Now what?"

"Now?" Theo had come up behind me and I twitched when he put his arms around me above Seth's arms and cupped both my breasts. "Now we get you naked and make you come repeatedly."

"I can't do multiple orgasms," I said.

"Seth and I love a good challenge," Theo said before licking the skin on my throat. I moaned and arched into his hands as Seth pulled on the hem of my shirt.

"Move for a minute, Theo."

Theo stepped away and Seth quickly pulled my shirt over my head and tossed it on the other bed.

"Fuck," he muttered as he stared at my tits. "Theo, get that fucking bra off."

The hooks on my bra were released with a quick flick of Theo's fingers and before I could think of protesting, it had joined my shirt. I reached to cover my breasts and Theo's fingers slid around my upper arms. He pulled my arms back, forcing my back to arch, and held me in a firm grip as Seth studied my breasts.

I wiggled and squirmed against Theo. His hot breath tickled my ear when he leaned down and said, "Hold still so Seth can see your tits or I'll spank your ass."

I twisted my head to stare at him and he kissed my mouth before sucking on my bottom lip. I moaned as he lifted his head. "Give us a safe word, Libby."

"Wh-what are you going to do to me?"

Seth laughed. "Nothing you won't enjoy, sweetheart, I promise. But Theo and I are dominant and we never play with a submissive unless she gives us a safe word."

"I'm not a submissive," I said.

"You still need a safe word, love," Theo said.

I hesitated as the sensible part of my brain started throwing out large neon caution signals.

"Libby," Seth said, "we promise we won't do anything you're not comfortable with. And if you are uncomfortable, say your safe word and we'll stop immediately."

"Do-do you promise?" I whispered.

"Yes," Theo said solemnly. "We promise."

"Okay, I guess, uh, red will be my safe word," I said. "Is that too cliché?"

Seth laughed and shook his head. "No, sweetheart, it's perfect."

Theo's hands tightened on my arms and I arched my back a little more.

"Good girl," Theo said.

Warmth flooded through me but before I could try and analyze why Theo's approval should make me feel so good, Seth was cupping both my breasts. He tugged on my nipples and I moaned and rubbed my ass against Theo's crotch. He pressed his erection against me as Seth said, "Her left tit is slightly bigger than her right one." He pulled on my nipples again and smiled when I gasped. "Her nipples seem to be very sensitive."

He cupped my breasts and lifted them. "Nice and heavy, just how we like them."

"Very nice," Theo said. He was looking over

my shoulder and I shivered when he nipped at my collarbone. "Show me her cunt."

Seth quickly unbuttoned and unzipped my jeans and yanked them down my legs. They dragged my panties with them and I squirmed a little when the cool air washed over my pussy. Theo dropped my arms but before I could move, he'd grabbed my wrists with one hand and held them in the small of my back.

He stepped back as Seth encouraged me to lift first one foot and than the other. He removed my shoes, my jeans, and my panties, and left them on the floor before straightening. I squirmed again. I was completely naked and neither Seth or Theo had even taken off their shoes.

"Fuck, her ass is amazing," Theo groaned.

I twitched when Theo's hand smoothed over the curve of my right ass cheek and then squeezed. "How does her cunt look?" He asked in a hoarse voice.

"Spread your legs, Libby," Seth said.

I kept my legs closed. Seth and Theo were examining my body almost like it was a piece of meat. I should have been insulted, I should have been safe wording and then telling them to get the hell out. Instead I was so turned on by the way they were treating me, I was afraid to open my legs because I was certain I'd drip all over the carpet. What was wrong with me?

I squealed when Theo slapped my ass. It hurt like hell and I turned my head and glared at him.

"Do what Seth says, love," Theo said calmly.

When I didn't spread my legs, Theo spanked my

ass again. This one hurt even more and I cried out and spread my legs wide.

"That's our good girl," Theo said. His big hand rubbed my stinging ass but I barely noticed. Seth had cupped my pussy the moment I spread my legs and his rough fingers were rubbing my clit.

"She's soaking wet already and her little clit is swollen and hard," he said in a low voice.

"Oh God, please," I moaned as he brushed the tips of his fingers over my clit.

Theo's hand stroked down my ass and slid between my legs. Seth spread my pussy lips apart and Theo rubbed at my clit before making a noise of approval.

I moaned and twisted against their hands and when Theo released my wrists, I grabbed Seth's shoulders in a desperate grip.

"Please, Seth," I pleaded. "I need – oh my God!"

I rose up on my tiptoes as two of Theo's thick fingers invaded my pussy. I clenched around him in surprise at the invasion and he groaned against my back. "Fuck, her cunt is tight."

He removed his fingers and I whimpered at the loss. He kissed the back of my shoulder as Seth cupped one heavy breast and pinched my nipple. My back arched and I squealed in surprise when I felt Theo's wet finger push against my anus.

"Hey!" I squeaked out.

Theo stopped and pressed another kiss against my shoulder. "Have you been fucked in the ass before, Libby?"

"No," I said.

A look of disappointment crossed Seth's face and I pressed my lips together. "I'm sorry." For some reason, I hated that I was disappointing him even though he was pretty much a stranger. "I'm willing to give it a try though."

Libby! You're going to let them fuck you in the ass? Sleeping with two men is one thing but do you really want to just have a go at the old DP? You haven't even seen their dicks yet – they're probably huge!

Seth smiled at me. "No, sweetheart, we can't."

"I – what? Why not?" I stuttered.

"Because you'll be too tight. You need to be stretched first before you take a cock, and that takes more than one night," Seth said.

I scowled at him. "It's my body and I'm willing to give it a try so – ouch! Goddammit! Why are you spanking me?"

Theo stopped with his hand hovering over my ass and said, "Seth told you no and you argued with him. You'll do what you're told or be punished."

"But it's my body! I can decide if I...shit!"

Theo had pulled me over to the bed. He sat on the side of it and I was sprawled face down over his lap before I knew what was happening. One hard hand splayed across my lower back, holding me down easily despite the way I was starting to wiggle. My face burned with humiliation and I squealed when Theo spanked me hard. I squirmed wildly but I was no match for his strength. As his hand painted my ass with bright red prints, I squealed again and said, "That hurts! Stop it!"

He ignored me completely, slapping each ass

cheek in a hard, unforgiving rhythm as Seth quickly undressed. Even with the burning pain and humiliation of being spanked, lust tinged with a little fear coursed through me when I saw the size of his dick.

I was distracted by another hard slap across my burning ass. Tears were beginning to slide down my face and I moaned at Theo to stop and tried to squirm away again. Why wasn't he stopping? I was practically begging him.

Safe word, idiot. If you want him to stop you have to use your safe word.

Fuck, I *was* an idiot. I opened my mouth to snap 'red' at Theo, but before I could say a word, he stopped spanking me and slipped his hand between my thighs. He rubbed my clit with a firm touch and all thoughts of safe wording disappeared in an instant. I had no idea if the pain had made me extra sensitive or if Theo was amazing at touching clits, but pleasure exploded in my belly. I cried out, my ass arching up and my hands clenching into the bedcovers as Seth grinned at Theo.

"Is she wet?"

Theo laughed. "Drenched. She loves being spanked."

"No, I don't!" I said. "I don't like it – oh fuck!"

Theo was spanking me again and tears streamed down my face as I wailed. He stopped spanking me and rubbed my sore ass with a light caress.

"Are you going to keep arguing with us, love?" He asked.

"No," I whimpered. "No, I – I won't."

"Good," Theo said. His hand slipped between my legs again and I moaned happily when he rubbed my clit. "Tell us that you're being a bad girl and deserve your spanking and we'll make you come."

I shook my head stubbornly. I wanted to come but I wasn't about to say that. It was one thing to be spanked and realize that it turned you on, but quite another to admit to being a bad girl and deserving a spanking. I was thirty-two years old, for God's sake. I wasn't going to –

"Libby," Theo's voice held a soft warning as he traced a finger over one red ass cheek, "be a good girl and do as I say."

I shook my head again and then moaned when Theo rubbed at my clit. Oh God, it felt so good. He knew the exact amount of pressure to use, the exact way to touch and –

"No!" I squealed when he stopped. I was right on the verge of my climax and I glared at him over my shoulder. "Theo, please!"

"Tell me what I want to hear," he said calmly.

I scowled at him and he laughed before giving me a quick spank to the ass. "I can deny you your orgasm all night, love."

"You wouldn't!" I gasped as he delved back between my legs and rubbed my clit again. This time he stroked too lightly to bring me to climax and I tried to rub myself against his hard thigh to find the relief I craved.

"Stop!" He said and slapped my ass again before returning to my clit.

"Oh God, oh God," I whispered. Within

minutes he had me writhing and moaning and pleading for relief. I was so close to my orgasm, I just needed a little more, but Theo refused to give it to me. He was no longer a dimpled god, but the dimpled devil and I was almost irrationally angry with him.

"Seth, please," I pleaded. He was standing close to us, stroking his cock and watching as Theo held me across his lap and tormented me. "Please tell him to make me come."

Seth laughed. "Be a good girl, sweetheart, and do what he says."

"Fuck!" I moaned. "I – I've been a bad girl and I deserve my spanking."

"That's my good girl," Theo said.

Another flush of warmth at his approval but I barely noticed it as Theo helped me stand. My legs were shaking and I was almost crying with the need for release.

"You promised!" I said. "You promised me!"

"Shh, love," Theo said as he stood next to me and kissed me on the forehead. "Seth is going to eat your sweet cunt for you."

"What? No!" I said as Theo turned me and pushed me into a sitting position on the bed. Seth moved forward and knelt next to the bed, his big hands grabbing my tightly-closed thighs and forcing them apart.

"No!" I said again. "I – I don't know you well enough to let you…"

I trailed off. Fuck, even I could hear how stupid I sounded. Seth laughed as Theo said, "You are delightful, sweet Libby."

"I think we should maybe get to know each other a little better before – oh my God!"

Seth had pulled my thighs wide and buried his face into my pussy. He licked at my swollen lips and then nibbled at them as my hands fisted in his hair. I moaned in disappointment when Seth lifted his head and grinned at Theo.

"How does she taste?" Theo was stripping off his shirt.

"Fucking delicious," Seth growled. He forced my legs over his shoulders and dived back into my wet pussy.

He reached up and cupped both of my breasts. He pulled hard on my nipples as his tongue finally found my throbbing clit. He licked it with light strokes and then sucked it into his mouth as he pinched both my nipples again.

I barely had time to throw my hand over my mouth before I was screaming with pleasure and coming all over his damn face. The orgasm tore through me, making my legs shake, my feet drum against his back and my entire body buck and heave. I had never come so hard in my life and I screamed against my palm for a second time as Seth raised his head and let my legs slip from his shoulders.

He stood up as Theo crowded in next to him. Now both men were naked and I stared at their erect cocks as Seth leaned down. "Sit up, sweetheart."

I was still shaking from my orgasm and wanted nothing more than to close my eyes and go to sleep but Seth wouldn't let me. He grasped my shoulders and helped me into a sitting position. Feeling weak and incredibly sated, I blinked up at them as Theo said, "She looks like a satisfied little kitten, doesn't she, Seth?"

He nodded and I blinked again when Theo's hand curved around the back of my skull. "Open up, little kitten."

The head of his cock pressed against my lips and I opened my mouth automatically. He slid his cock between my lips and made a harsh groan. "Suck, Libby."

I sucked on the head of his cock, sliding my tongue back and forth over the tip before tracing the ridge. He moaned and pressed forward. His cock was huge and I could feel my lips stretching as he fed me more of his dick. I made a muffled sound of protest and he petted my hair.

"I won't give you too much, Libby. Relax for me."

I did what he asked and he petted my hair again as I bobbed my head back and forth over his cock.

"Look up at me, Libby."

I stared up at him as I sucked and he nodded. "That's my good girl. Always look at me when you're sucking my dick."

"Theo," Seth said hoarsely.

"I'm being greedy, little Libby," Theo said. He pulled back and I released his cock with a soft pop and licked my already swollen lips. He turned my head to the right and I stared at Seth's cock.

This time I didn't have to be told what to do. I opened my mouth and stared obediently at Seth as I took his cock into my mouth and sucked hard. The two men were similar in length and width but Seth had a slightly saltier taste than Theo. I realized that I actually loved the way they both tasted and I licked at the head of Seth's cock as precum dripped out of the slit.

"Oh fuck," Seth groaned.

Theo's hand was still cupping the back of my skull and he held me in place as Seth pushed forward. His cock brushed against the back of my throat and I made another muffled noise of protest.

"We want to see how much you can take, sweetheart," Seth said. "Be a good girl and open wide."

I did what he asked despite my sudden real fear of choking on Seth's giant dick. He pushed forward even more, cutting off my oxygen and making my eyes water as I sucked. He pulled out and I took a deep gasping breath as Seth wiped away the moisture leaking from my eyes.

"Good girl," he said. "You're doing so well."

My head was turned back toward Theo and I accepted his cock without protest.

"Have you deep throated a guy before, Libby?" Theo asked.

I shook my head around his cock and gave him a wary look as he pushed further in. He smiled reassuringly at me. "I'm not going to force you to deepthroat me, but you are going to try very hard and take as much as you can. Aren't you, love?"

I stared up at him and he pulled out and rubbed the head of his cock against my lips. "Aren't you?"

"Yes," I whispered.

"Yes, what?"

I thought for a moment before licking my

swollen lips again. "Yes, Sir."

His and Seth's smiles of approval made my clit pulse with need and I squeezed my thighs together as Seth said, "We're going to fuck your mouth, sweetheart. If it's too much and you can't safe word because you've got one of our dicks in your mouth, tap me twice on the hip. Okay?"

"Okay," I whispered.

"Good. Open up, Libby," Theo said.

I opened wide and Theo slid his cock into my mouth. I sucked and licked and tried to relax my throat as Theo groaned under his breath and pulled on my hair. After a few minutes, Seth took his place. I lost track of time as they took turns fucking my mouth. Whoever didn't have their dick in my mouth, crooned soft words of encouragement and cupped and kneaded my breasts, playing with my nipples until I was rubbing my ass and pussy against the bed in a silent plea for relief.

"She looks like she needs to come again," Seth said to Theo.

"Fuck, I need to come too," Theo muttered. "Do you want her pussy or her mouth?"

"Pussy," Seth said immediately as he watched his cock disappear into my mouth.

When he pulled out and walked away, I whined in protest. Theo lifted me to my feet and pressed a kiss against my swollen mouth. "He's getting a condom, love."

"Please fuck me," I whispered.

I couldn't believe how turned on I was. I'd always been enthusiastic about giving Wayne blowjobs – I loved a dick in my mouth as much as the next girl – but sucking Wayne's dick had never made me so wet I was dripping. Especially when I'd already had an unbelievable orgasm not half an hour earlier.

Yeah, well, Wayne's dick was nothing to write home about and it wasn't like he was all that great about returning the favour.

My inner voice had a point. Wayne loved blowjobs but wasn't as enthusiastic about giving me oral. I thought about the way Seth had eaten my pussy, how he had dived in like I was a bowl of his favourite ice cream, and my pussy pulsed with need. Liquid dripped down my thighs as Theo said, "Get on your hands and knees."

Feeling a little embarrassed, I climbed up on the bed and settled onto my hands and knees. Wayne had two positions he stuck with – missionary and me on top – and I'd been too young and shy to experiment much with boyfriends before Wayne. Still, I wasn't about to tell the two hot naked men in my hotel room that I'd never been fucked doggy style before so I tried to look like I knew what I was doing as Theo urged me to the middle of the bed.

I watched as Seth rolled on a condom before kneeling behind me on the bed. His hard hands stroked my tender ass and I winced. He pressed a kiss on my lower back.

"Is your ass sore, sweetheart?"

"Yes," I said a bit snottily.

He laughed and gave my ass a light slap. "Maybe next time you'll be quicker to obey us."

I didn't reply. There wouldn't be a next time. As much as I was enjoying this night, I couldn't sleep with two men on a regular basis. That wasn't me. I didn't do stuff like this on a regular night for God's sake.

"Libby, look at me."

I turned forward as the bed dipped. Theo was standing next to the bed in front of me and his cock was directly in front of my mouth. I leaned forward, my lips already parting as Theo gathered my hair into a loose ponytail. His other hand stroked the back of my neck and he guided my mouth over his dick. I sucked with enthusiasm, staring up at him as he held me by my hair.

I pulled my mouth away when I felt the head of Seth's dick press against my opening. I looked over my shoulder, feeling the pull against my scalp when Theo refused to release my hair.

"You're, um, bigger than I'm used to. Will you go slow?" I asked. I sounded timid and unsure even to myself. Gratitude flooded through me when both men immediately stroked my body with their warm hands and made soothing noises.

"I will," Seth said as his big hands rubbed my lower back. "Spread your legs wider, sweetheart."

I did what he asked and stared up at Theo again as he smoothed my hair back from my face before gathering it into a ponytail again. "If you can't safe word, two taps on my hip. Remember, love?"

I nodded and he leaned down and kissed my mouth. "Good girl. You're going to love this, I promise."

I expected him to push his dick into my mouth again but instead he glanced up at Seth. "Give her your dick. I want to watch her face as she takes it."

I tried not to tense when Seth pushed the head of his cock into my narrow entrance. He made a low moan as Theo studied my face intently. Seth's rough fingers trailed across my hip and I sucked in my gut when they crossed my stomach.

He made a low grunt of disapproval and I flinched when he slapped me sharply on the ass. "Don't do that, Libby."

I licked my lips and tried to take Theo's cock into my mouth. What better way to distract myself from the giant dick about to invade my pussy than with a giant dick in my mouth, right? Unfortunately, Theo wouldn't let me and I pouted at him as Seth's hand slid underneath me.

"I want your cock in my mouth." I blushed at my boldness but Theo shook his head.

"Not yet, love. And next time add a 'Sir' to your request or you'll get another spanking."

I didn't reply. Seth's fingers were brushing my clit and I had lost all interest in Theo's dick. I squirmed on Seth's hand, panting and pleading quietly as he stroked the sensitive nub. I was close to coming when I felt Seth's dick push into my pussy. This time I pushed back eagerly. My clit was throbbing and my pussy was clenching uselessly around nothing and wanted what Seth was offering. Seth surged forward and Theo pulled my head back with a tight grip on my hair. He studied my face as Seth forced my pussy to take every inch of his dick.

My mouth dropped open and I whimpered as I struggled to take all of it. When he was completely sheathed, he stopped and rubbed my lower back. I moaned and tried to wiggle away from the invasion. My inner walls were stretching around him, but it was still more discomfort than I was used to from sex. Seth's hands cupped my hips and held me firmly as Theo smiled at me.

"How does it feel, Libby?"

"Too big," I said stupidly.

He laughed and tugged on my hair. "Open your mouth."

I opened my mouth and took Theo's cock when he pushed it past my lips. Seth began a slow slide and retreat motion as Theo used my hair to glide my mouth back and forth over his cock. I moaned and clenched around Seth's dick when he rubbed my clit.

"Fuck!" Seth muttered. "She's goddamn tight, Theo."

"Fuck her hard," Theo suddenly demanded.

My squeal of surprise was muffled around Theo's cock as Seth immediately began to fuck me with rough thrusts. His fingers rubbed at my clit as Theo's hand pulled at my hair. The sting in my scalp, the way Seth's cock stretched my pussy, and the feel of his fingers against my sensitive clit were lighting up my nerve endings like a goddamn Christmas tree. Both men were groaning now and they were losing their smooth, natural rhythm.

As Theo shoved his cock deep into my mouth, he groaned, "Fuck, I'm gonna come. Make her come first."

Seth's fingers rubbed furiously at my clit as he pounded into my pussy. My back arched, I screamed around Theo's thick cock and came in a roaring rush of pleasure that blotted out all rational thought. Theo pulled his dick out of my mouth and yanked my head back by my hair. He made a low growl of pleasure as he pumped his dick with his hand and came all over my throat and chest. Still shaking with my climax, I cried out when Seth's hands clamped down on my hips and he shoved himself in deep. He did short and hard strokes until he made his own roar of pleasure and his big body tensed. He jerked against my ass, panting harshly as he came deep inside of me.

Theo released my hair and I wanted to fall flat on my face, but he steadied me with one hand on my shoulder. "Seth, lift her up."

He disappeared from view as Seth wrapped his arm around my waist and hauled me up until I was on my knees. He was still inside of me and made a few gentle thrusts as he cupped my breast and kissed my cheek.

"You're so beautiful, Libby," he whispered into my ear. "Beautiful and tight and so fucking submissive. Do you have any idea how badly I want to put a collar around your neck and clamps on your beautiful nipples?"

His fingers pulled at my right nipple. Surprisingly, a little shiver of need went down my spine even as my body was still shaking from my orgasm. What the hell was wrong with me?

Before I could answer my question, Theo had returned. He was carrying a towel from the bathroom and he wiped away his cum from my throat and chest before dropping the towel on the floor.

"How do you feel, love?"

"Really, really good," I mumbled. "You guys are really, really good at sex."

Seth laughed and kissed my cheek again before pulling out of me. I swayed on my knees and Theo helped me off the bed before pulling back the covers. "Climb in, Libby."

I wondered if they were going to leave. Was I supposed to ask them to stay or was that weird? I'd never had a one-night stand before. I assumed that I would find a guy, fuck him, and the guy would leave. But here I was with two men and wishing desperately they would crawl into bed and snuggle with me.

Before I could make a fool of myself and ask, Theo was crawling into the bed behind me. He curved his body around mine and cupped my pussy before kissing my neck. "This is our pussy. Say it, Libby."

"It's your pussy," I said obediently. Whether I believed it or not, didn't matter I supposed. There was no harm in saying what they wanted to hear. I'd never see either of them again after tonight.

Seth slid into the bed on my other side and I smiled at him when he rested his head on the pillow next to mine before kissing the tip of my nose. "Have I mentioned you're beautiful, Libby?"

"Thank you. So are you," I said before yawning.

He laughed and cupped my right tit, giving the nipple a little pinch. "Our sweet cunt and our tits. Right?"

"Right," I said. "All yours."

I was so sleepy, I could barely keep my eyes open. It was dangerous to fall asleep with two men I didn't know, but it didn't feel dangerous to me. It felt good and normal and...*right*. As Seth and Theo pushed in close, their hard bodies cocooning me in warmth, I closed my eyes and slept.

Chapter Three

I studied my reflection in the mirror on the back of my bedroom door. I straightened the skirt of my dark green suit and adjusted the collar before smoothing back a stray strand of hair. I had put my dark hair up in a twist, maintaining a look of competent and easy sophistication. My makeup was minimal with just a bit of blush, mascara and a tinted lip gloss. A plain silver bangle around my wrist and pearl drop earrings finished my outfit.

I grabbed my heels out of my suitcase and bent to pick up my cell phone from where it was plugged in next to the air mattress. Yesterday morning, I had picked up the key to the townhouse I rented but a storm had stranded the moving truck carrying my stuff. The representative from the moving company couldn't even give me an estimate of when my things would arrive. Her vague warning that it might not be until after Christmas had turned my blood cold.

Thankfully I had packed enough work clothes to last me the week I'd be at the office before the

Christmas holidays started, so I didn't need to buy clothes. However, clothes and toiletries were the only things I had packed in my car. I had already checked out of the hotel and while I could have rented a room again, I decided to pick up a few supplies to camp out at the townhouse. I bought groceries, an air mattress, pillows and bedding and hauled it up to my townhouse, setting it up in the master bedroom on Sunday afternoon. I had an early dinner and a couple of glasses of wine. My mother had called twice and I let both calls go to voicemail. Feeling nervous and anxious about my first day, I went to bed early.

Now, I checked my reflection again and turned to glance at my ass. I smoothed my skirt over it and then winced. God, my ass was still sore. Even this morning there were visible handprints on it.

I blushed furiously and left the bedroom. I slipped into my boots and grabbed my coat from the front closet before stuffing my heels and my phone into my oversized bag. With my coffee maker stuck in a moving truck, I wanted to leave early to find a coffee shop. I locked the door and hurried down the sidewalk to my parking spot. The morning air was cold, the sky dark with grey, ominous looking clouds, and I could almost taste the snow that was going to fall.

I unlocked my car and sat down behind the wheel, wincing again when my sore ass met the seat. I would need to make a concentrated effort not to flinch when I sat at the office. I started the car and turned the heater to high, rubbing my hands together briskly. As I waited for the car to warm, I couldn't help but think about Saturday night. I had tried and failed miserably not to think about Theo and Seth yesterday. But today, I should have been concentrating on my new job, not wishing for about the fiftieth time that I hadn't thrown away Theo's cell number. I sighed, my warm breath clouding the cold air as I stared blankly out the windshield and my mind drifted back to yesterday.

Theo and Seth woke me around four in the morning with their warm mouths and hard hands. Half asleep, I hadn't protested when they kissed and touched me into another unbelievably aching arousal. I climbed to my hands and knees again and this time sucked on Seth's cock as Theo fucked me from behind. Theo was maybe a tiny bit larger than Seth, but he had rubbed and caressed my clit until I was soaking wet and it seemed a little easier to take his dick than Seth's. Like before, I'd had a crazy intense orgasm that left me shaking and weak as a kitten. Theo and Seth tucked me back into bed and we'd slept again until Seth shook me awake at ten.

"We have to go, sweetheart," he said as he sat on the side of the bed.

I sat up and clutched the sheets to my naked chest. Seth was fully dressed and Theo was finishing dressing. He pulled his boots on and sat on the other side of me as I blinked owlishly at them.

"I – what time is it?" I asked.

"Just after ten," Theo said. He leaned forward and pressed a kiss against my bare shoulder. "We had a great time last night, Libby. Thank you."

Suddenly feeling shy, I glanced at my hands

twisting in my lap. "I did too. Thank you."

Seth tipped my chin up before planting a soft kiss against my lips. "We'd like to see you again."

"What?" I stared at him in surprise and he grinned.

"We want to see you again. Will you have dinner with us this week?"

"Oh, um, I don't... I mean, I'm starting a new job and it's the holidays and I'm kind of busy," I said.

Libby! What is wrong with you? Say yes!

"Fair enough," Theo said as he pressed another kiss against my shoulder. "I've left my cell number written down on the pad of paper on the desk. Call or text me if you'd like to have dinner with us after the holidays. Okay?"

"Uh, sure, okay," I said.

Seth smiled at me. "Good bye, Libby. It was great to meet you, I hope to see you again soon."

"Bye, Seth," I whispered.

He pressed a kiss against my mouth and stood as Theo leaned in and kissed me as well. Both men headed toward the door and hesitated for a moment, glancing at each other.

"Bye, Libby," Theo finally said.

"Bye."

They left, shutting the door behind them and I collapsed on the bed for a moment before hopping out and heading to the bathroom. I peed and then brushed my teeth and had a long hot shower before dressing. My ass hurt and my body was aching but I felt strangely satisfied and the pain in my ass almost made me proud.

I sighed and packed my suitcase before staring fixedly at the piece of paper with Theo's number written on it. Last night was amazing and I'd enjoyed it a great deal, but I couldn't see them again. It was a one-time thing, a 'get your mojo back' moment and besides, I couldn't date two men at once. Nice girls didn't do that sort of thing and if anyone at the office were to find out, I'd die of shame. I shuddered at the thought and immediately crumpled up the paper and tossed it into the trash before grabbing my suitcase and nearly running out of the room. I was a new partner at a new firm, I needed to concentrate on doing my damn job instead of having a fling with two playboy construction workers. No matter how good they made me feel.

The shrill ring of my cell phone brought me back to the present and I fumbled my phone out of my purse. Caught up in my memories of yesterday, I almost believed that it would be Theo or Seth calling me. I was being stupid. They didn't have my number and they didn't even know my last name. I checked the number and sighed before answering it.

"Hi, Mom."

"Elizabeth! I tried calling you twice last night and you didn't answer. Are you okay? I've been worried sick."

"I'm fine, Mom," I said as I put her on speaker and set my phone on the seat. I pulled out of my parking spot and turned right onto the street. "I went to bed early last night."

"I was so worried about you."

"You need to stop worrying. The city is very safe."

"Are you unpacked yet?"

I grimaced. "My stuff has been delayed because of a snowstorm."

"Oh my God! What are you doing to do?"

"I bought an air mattress and I'm camping out in my townhouse," I said. I caught glimpse of a Starbucks sign and muttered a quiet 'thank god' as I drove toward it. I turned into the parking lot and headed toward the drive-thru.

"Your Aunt Leona called yesterday. Apparently, Uncle Bert was caught with his pants down at the store with their newest employee. You remember Jolene, don't you? She's only forty-five years old but apparently, she likes older men because Leona said she and Bert were having sex in the storage room like a couple of randy teenagers! Bert is sixty-eight years old. Can you imagine it?"

"Mom," I said as I waited in line, "can we talk about Uncle Bert's sex life later? I'm on my way to my new job and I'm a little nervous."

"You should be nervous," my mother said. "Being a partner is a big responsibility and I'm not sure you're quite ready for it."

I tried not to let her words sting. "Thanks for the vote of confidence."

"You need someone who will be truthful to you," she snapped. "Don't be angry with me because I'm trying to keep you from making a fool of yourself."

"I'm not angry," I said. "But I do have to go. I'll call you later."

"Fine," my mother huffed. "Goodbye, Elizabeth."

My cell phone beeped as she ended the call and I sighed and rubbed my forehead as I inched forward in the drive-thru line. I wished to God I had never answered her call and I tried to forget what she had said as I rolled my window down and placed my order. Today would go fine. I was a damn good lawyer and I deserved to be partner. Absolutely nothing would go wrong today.

&~ ~&

"Elizabeth!" Jeff Martin, the head partner at Martin, Clarke and Bones, strolled into my office. I stood and he shook my hand with a hard grip. "How's your first morning going?"

"Call me Libby," I said. "It's going well. IT already had my system set up and ready to go and Sandra has been a real-life saver in familiarizing me with the computer system."

"Excellent," Jeff said. "Sandra is one of our best legal assistants in the office. I had a feeling the two of you would get along which is why I assigned her to you. Now, if you have a minute, I've asked everyone in the office to come to the boardroom. There's coffee and snacks there, and we'll formally introduce you to the rest of the staff."

"Sounds good," I said. I took a deep breath and followed Jeff to the boardroom. It was crowded with people and I smiled at the other two head partners, Emmett Clark and Mario Bones. I had met with all three partners during negotiations for partnership and liked all of them. Jeff and I joined them at the front of the room and I shook both their hands before standing next to Mario.

Jeff cleared his throat and clapped his hands. The murmur of voices quieted and Jeff said, "Is everyone here, Wanda?"

"Almost," a small chubby woman said from the back. "Seth and Theo are at a client, but they should be back any minute."

I jerked and Mario gave me a curious look. "Are you okay, Elizabeth?"

"Call me Libby," I said automatically. Wanda hadn't said Seth and Theo, of course she hadn't. I was hearing things because I was suddenly obsessed with two damn construction workers who had giant dicks and an almost magical ability to make me come.

"We'll start without them," Jeff said. "Everyone, I'd like to formally introduce you to Elizabeth Brecken, our newest associate partner. She comes to us from – ah, Seth, Theo, you made it. Come on in."

I stared at the two men who had entered the boardroom. My face paled and my stomach rolled with nausea as they gave each other identical grins of delight. I swallowed down the bile and stared straight ahead, keeping a smile on my face by sheer willpower alone. Seth and Theo, the two men who had spanked me, ate my pussy and fucked me into multiple orgasms the night before last, were goddamn lawyers at my goddamn firm.

Fuck me.

⁊ ⁊

An hour later, I was back at my desk and grimly staving off the panic that was gnawing at my guts. I had met almost all of my coworkers at the gathering, but I couldn't remember a single one of their names. Nor could I remember Jeff's introductory speech. I know he kept it short and simple. I know he mentioned my experience and the client I brought with me to the firm, but only because a few of the lawyers had mentioned it to me when we chatted. At least, I think they did. I'd been so busy trying to not freak the fuck out that I couldn't be sure of anything. The only thing I did know, is that Seth and Theo had slipped out of the boardroom without talking to me and I was stupidly grateful. I had no idea what to say to them and pretending that I didn't know them would have been impossible with my current level of shock.

I spun around in my chair and stared out the window at the falling snow. Okay, everything was fine. So, two guys that I fucked happened to be my new coworkers. No big deal. We were all adults, right?

They're not just coworkers, Libby, inner me moaned. *You're their boss! You fucked two subordinates! What if they blackmail you? What if they threaten to tell the other partners?*

Oh God, what the fuck was I going to do? My panic pushed to the front and feeling half-crazed, I jumped to my feet. I had to tell the other partners what happened before Seth and Theo told them. It was better coming from me, I rationalized as I crossed my office.

Libby no! You can't tell them you fucked Seth

and Theo! You're the only woman partner at this firm, and if you tell them what you did, you can kiss your career goodbye! They'll never look at you the same again. You know they won't!

"I have to do something!" I hissed to the empty room. "I can't just sit here and – and…"

I trailed off as there was a knock on my door and it opened. Jeff stepped into my office and my stomach dropped when Seth and Theo followed him in.

"Hello, Elizabeth," Jeff said.

I smiled at him but said nothing. If I opened my mouth I was very certain I would throw up on his fucking shoes.

"I don't think you got the chance to meet Seth and Theo so I wanted to bring them to you. They'll be working directly with you on your client, Etco Drilling Ltd."

No! Oh fuck me, no!

I remained silent and Jeff gave me an odd look before turning to Seth and Theo. "Elizabeth, meet Seth Waters and Theo Camden."

Theo stepped toward me and held out his hand. He gave me an encouraging look and my hand trembling, I took his. He shook it quickly. "It's nice to meet you, Elizabeth."

"You too," I said in a low voice as I turned to Seth.

"Hi, Libby. Nice to meet you," he said before shaking my hand.

"How do you know she's a Libby?" Jeff asked as both men stepped away from me.

I almost moaned out loud with sheer terror but

Seth simply grinned and shrugged. "She looks like a Libby. Am I right?"

"Yes," I said. My voice came out squeaky and I cleared my throat as Jeff gave me a look of concern.

"Are you all right, Elizabeth? You're very pale."

"Fine," I said. For a moment, I thought about blurting out exactly what I had done with Seth and Theo, but my common sense kicked in and I kept my mouth shut.

"All right. Well, I'll let you three get acquainted," Jeff said. "Seth, come see me after about the Moranis file."

"Of course," Seth said.

Jeff left the office and closed the door. As soon as it was shut, Theo grinned at me. "Hello again, Libby."

I didn't reply and Seth gave me a wicked little grin. "You have no idea how happy we are to see you again."

I staggered back and their flirty grins dropped away.

"Libby?" Theo was reaching for me and I tried to pull back, but my legs were shaking badly and I stumbled into him instead. He steadied me and muttered 'shit' under his breath before leading me to the small couch in the corner of my office.

I collapsed in an ungraceful heap on it and Theo glanced at Seth. "Grab some water, would you?"

"Libby, are you okay?" Theo asked as he sat next to me. Seth walked to the credenza behind my desk, grabbed a bottle of water and returned. He sat down on the couch on my other side - it was a tight fit for the three of us - and opened the bottle of water before handing it to me.

"Drink, sweetheart."

My hands were still shaking, and Theo muttered another curse before helping guide the water bottle to my mouth. I drank a few swallows and then pushed it away. I stared mutely at Theo and Seth as Theo said, "Better?"

"You're supposed to be construction workers," I said.

Seth blinked at me. "What?"

"You – your hands are so rough and your clothes were covered in paint and sawdust. You're labourers, not lawyers," I whispered.

Theo glanced at Seth. "We're doing our renovations on our house, Libby. It's why we looked the way we did Saturday night."

"Oh God, oh no," I groaned before burying my hands in my face. "What have I done?"

"It's no big deal," Seth said.

I lifted my head. "No big deal? No big fucking deal? I'm your goddamn boss, Seth! I'm your boss and I let you spank me and – and fuck me and…"

I trailed off and buried my face in my hands again. Theo rubbed my lower back. "You didn't know who we were, Libby."

"Did you know who I was?" I lifted my head again as I had a sudden thought. "Did you fucking plan this? Get the boss into our bed so we can – can blackmail her?"

"Christ, no," Seth said. "Sweetheart, how would we know who you were?"

"You knew there was a new associate partner

coming in," I snapped.

"Yes," Theo said patiently. "We knew there was an associate partner named Elizabeth Brecken. But we didn't know what you looked like and you introduced yourself at the bar as Libby."

"Libby is a common nickname for Elizabeth," I retorted.

"We didn't know who you were. We swear it, love," Theo said.

"Don't call me that," I whispered. "I'm your boss."

"Sorry," Theo said immediately. "But we honestly didn't know who you were."

I studied him before nodding. "Yeah, okay, I believe you."

"Good," Theo said. "Drink some more water. You're very shaky."

I drank a couple more swallows of water before staring at my hands. "So, now what?"

Seth shrugged. "We're not going to say anything to anyone at the office, if that's what you mean. We keep our personal lives private, Libby."

"I appreciate that," I said, "but I meant more about the fact that we're supposed to work on the Etco file together. You know Jeff better than I do, would he find it strange if I asked for you both to be reassigned?"

"Why would you do that?" Theo said. "Seth and I are good at what we do and we're the only lawyers in the firm who have some experience with drilling companies."

I gaped at him. "Why – why would I do that? Have you lost your damn mind?"

"I don't think so," Theo said.

"I let you spank me!" I hissed at him. "I called you Sir and sucked your dick and you're wondering why I don't want to work with you? I've lost all credibility with you both. Can you honestly tell me that you can take orders from a woman who you put across your lap and spanked? I still have your goddam handprints on my ass!"

A small smile crossed Theo's face and I shoved him in the chest. "This is not fucking funny!"

"I apologize," Theo said. "I know it's not funny, Libby."

"Libby, listen to us," Seth said. "We're only dominant with a woman in the bedroom. We have no problem following your orders in the office, I promise. We can keep what happened in bed between us completely separate from our office lives."

"Maybe you can," I said dully, "but I don't think I can."

"You can," Theo said. "You're a bright, capable woman and from what we've heard, a damn good lawyer. Just because you're submissive in bed doesn't mean you can't do your job."

"I'm not submissive in bed," I said.

Theo and Seth glanced at each other over my head and I groaned. "Oh God, I should never have gone to the bar."

"But you did and you can't change that," Seth said. "Listen, it will look strange to Jeff if you ask for us to be reassigned without even working with us. Can you give it a try? There's no harm in that and if, after a couple of weeks, it isn't working, then you can talk to Jeff about reassigning us."

I studied both of them before straightening. I was a good lawyer and I was a natural leader when it came to work. I tried to sound like my usual authoritative self. "It has to be completely professional. At all times. If I even think you're looking at me in a way that might suggest you're remembering what I looked like naked, I'll ask Jeff to reassign you. Do you understand?"

"We do," Theo said.

"Good." I stood and moved to my desk. My legs were still trembling, but I kept my back straight and gave them a polite and professional smile. "It was nice to meet you both. I look forward to working with you."

A goddamn lie, but if this was going to work I had to make myself believe that I had never seen them naked, never had their dicks in my mouth and my pussy. The only way to do that was to shove those memories right out of my head and pretend that they were total strangers.

I sat down at my desk and stared at my laptop as Seth said, "This will work, Libby. I promise."

"I'm sure it will," I said with an indifference I didn't feel. "Unless you have any specific questions about Etco, you're dismissed."

I glanced up at them as they moved toward the door. They didn't seem put off by my coolness as they left my office. The second the door was closed, I slumped in my chair and rubbed at my temples.

Oh God, I was so fucking screwed.

Chapter Four

Tuesday night I was walking through the door of my townhouse when my cell phone rang. I kicked off my boots and pulled my phone out of my purse as I shrugged out of my coat.

"Hey, Sandra. What's up?"

"Hi, Libby. Are you home yet?" My legal assistant's voice was apologetic.

"I am, why?" I asked.

"You were going to work on the Henden file tonight, right?"

"Yes," I said.

"It's sitting on my desk."

"Crap," I muttered. "Okay, I'm headed back to the office now."

"Don't do that," Sandra said. "There are still a few people at the office, I'm sure I can find someone to drop it off for you on their way home."

"I don't want to put anyone out," I said. "I'll come back to the office and - "

"It's fine," Sandra replied. "Don't worry about it, Libby."

"Thanks, Sandra. I appreciate it." I ended the call and tossed my phone on the counter before dropping my workbag at my feet.

It was only my second day but I already had a full client list. Not that I minded. I needed something to take my mind off of Seth and Theo. Just the thought of them made my pussy damp, and I cursed my libido as I headed to the bedroom and changed into yoga pants and a t-shirt. I hadn't seen them at all since Monday and I told myself repeatedly that it was a good thing. The less I had to do with them, the better.

So why had I spent most of last night tossing and turning on my stupid air mattress? Why couldn't I stop thinking about what they had done to me and how it had made me feel? And why did I finally have to masturbate just to fall asleep?

Not that it helped, I thought as I headed back to the kitchen. I could barely concentrate on my new job and I was furious with myself over it. It's like I was trying to sabotage my own damn career, and for what? The possibility of getting fucked by two men at once? Since when did my need for sex override my desire to have a fulfilling career?

Why not have both? Inner me whispered slyly. *You can have your cake and eat it too, Libby.*

No, I couldn't. Especially not with two of my coworkers. It didn't matter how damn hot they were or how easily they made me come. Nothing good would come of sleeping with them, and trying to talk myself into it not being a problem, was a career ending move.

They said they can keep it separate. You can

too. Simple.

"No, it isn't simple," I said to my empty kitchen. "It isn't simple at all."

You suck, my inner voice pouted.

I ignored it and pulled my laptop out of my workbag. I needed to concentrate on my career and pretend like I had no idea what Seth and Theo's dicks looked like. Easy. Simple. Doable.

You know who else is doable?

I made a harsh groan of frustration and yanked open my laptop. I was going insane.

∂⁕ ⅏

Half an hour later, I cursed and nearly pounded my fists against my laptop. I had wasted thirty minutes looking for an answer to a question that had already been answered. I wanted to scream in anger. Never before had I questioned my abilities as a lawyer, but if I couldn't stop thinking about what it would be like to have Seth and Theo both inside of me at once, I could kiss my damn career goodbye.

I took a deep breath and rubbed my temples before taking a bite of cereal. Okay, I was overreacting. My entire career wasn't on the precipice of collapse just because I was horny. There was a simple solution to this whole damn mess. Hit up another bar this weekend and find a guy – *one guy* – to have sex with. That would help with the horniness and make me forget all about Seth and Theo. Right?

Nope. So wrong, girl. So. Very. Wrong.

I wasn't wrong. Wayne might have crushed my

sexual self-esteem with one sentence but Seth and Theo had at least brought a little of it back. It was enough for me to have the courage to find someone else to have sex with. Maybe I could fuck away my memories of my two coworkers.

I rubbed my back as I shifted from foot to foot. I don't know why I didn't stay at the damn office and work on the Henden file. I'd received an email this morning from the moving company that my furniture was definitely stranded until after the New Year. I didn't even have a kitchen table or chairs which meant I was trying to work standing at the counter. I ate another bite of cereal. Tomorrow I would stay at the office until I was finished work. It made the most sense.

The doorbell rang and I crunched down another bite of cereal as I headed down the front hallway. I opened the door, the smile dropping from my face.

"What are you doing here?" I asked.

Theo held up the manila covered file folder as Seth smiled at me. "Dropping off the Henden file."

I stared silently at them and Theo said, "Sandra said you needed it and your place is close to ours."

"It is?" I ignored the dirty thoughts that immediately coursed through my head.

"Yes," Seth said. "We told Sandra we would be happy to drop off the file for you."

"You live together?" I said.

"We do," Theo replied.

"Okay, well, thanks for dropping off the file." Ignoring my mad idea to invite them in, I reached for the folder, but Theo refused to relinquish it.

"Invite us in, Libby."

"Why?" I said.

"Because I'm freezing my nutsack off standing out here and Seth has to pee."

I bit back my smile as Seth said, "It's true. I have to pee."

Knowing it was insanity, I took a step back and said, "Come in."

"Thanks, Libby," Theo said.

He and Seth stepped into the hallway and there was a moment of awkwardness before I said, "Um, the guest bathroom is down the hallway to the right."

"Perfect." Seth headed to the bathroom and I took the file from Theo.

"Thanks for bringing this by," I said. I pulled self-consciously at my t-shirt as Theo smiled at me.

"You're welcome. Hey, can I grab a glass of water from you?"

"Yeah, uh, okay."

He followed me into the kitchen. I wondered if he was staring at my ass as I opened the fridge and grabbed a bottle of water for him.

"Here you go…what's wrong?"

Theo was staring at my kitchen. "Don't take this the wrong way, Libby, but if you're a minimalist, I think you've taken it too far."

I laughed. "I'm not, I just - "

"Whoa," Seth had joined us in the kitchen. "You know most people have a table in their kitchen, right, Libs?"

"I'm aware," I said dryly. "The moving truck with all of my furniture and belongings is stranded about four hours from here. I won't get it until after the New Year."

"Jesus, that sucks," Theo said. "Why don't you rent a hotel room?"

"It's not that bad."

"Is that why you're eating cold cereal out of a Styrofoam bowl?" Seth asked. He crossed the kitchen and peered at my bowl of cereal.

"Yeah," I said. "I didn't want to buy new kitchen stuff just to cook food for a couple of weeks and eating at a restaurant alone isn't my thing."

"Do you even have a bed?" Theo asked.

I immediately blushed but he didn't seem to notice as he twisted open the cap on his water and took a drink. "I have an air mattress."

"Well that fucking sucks," he replied.

"It's not that bad," I said.

"I have a great idea," Seth said. "We live like ten minutes from here. Come back to our place and I'll cook you dinner."

"Hell, no," I said. "That is not happening."

"Why not?" Theo said.

"You know why not," I replied.

Seth shrugged. "We can keep it professional if you can."

"Of course I can!" I snapped at him.

Fuck, could I?

"Then it isn't a problem to have dinner with us."

"I have to work on the Henden file," I said.

"Bring it with you," Theo said. "We have a home office. You use the office to work while Seth cooks dinner. Come on, Libby. It's a lot easier than standing at your counter and Seth is an amazing cook. He'll make something much better than cold cereal, I guarantee it."

I couldn't say yes, no matter what my libido was screaming.

"No one from the office will find out," Seth said. "We're the only three who live in the west end of the city. No one will know you're at our house."

I couldn't go to their house. I couldn't. I took a deep breath and said, "Sure, okay."

Libby!

"Great!" Theo gave me a boyish grin that made the butterflies in my stomach start up. "Grab your jacket and we'll give you a ride over to - "

"No," I interrupted. "I'll drive myself over."

"All right," Theo said. "Let's get out of here."

ॐ ॐ

"Hey, how's it going in here?" Theo stuck his head into the office as I was closing my laptop.

"Good. I'm done."

"Perfect timing," Theo said. "Dinner is ready."

I stood and tried not to notice the way Theo's gaze dropped to my tits. I was still wearing my t-shirt and yoga pants. I had thought about changing into something a little more flattering before berating myself internally. I shouldn't care what I looked like around Seth and Theo.

I followed him out of the office and down the hallway. They'd given me a brief tour of their house when we first arrived, pointing out the renovations they'd done. I was genuinely impressed. They had gutted and remodeled the kitchen themselves as well as their bedrooms, the office and all three of the bathrooms. They were currently working on the guest bedroom and in the spring, would start the living room.

"Have a seat, Libs," Seth said as he pointed to the large marble island. Plates and silverware were already in place and I climbed onto the stool as Theo moved to the fridge.

"Do you want wine?"

"No, just water, please," I said. There was no way in hell I was having anything to drink around these two. I was already turned on and wanting to beg them to fuck me. If I had even a drop of liquor, I was deathly afraid I'd lose the tenuous grip on my control.

I took a deep breath and drank some of the water that Theo handed me. Surprisingly, I could focus enough to get my damn work done. I had thought it would be impossible but apparently just being near the two men, soothed me enough to concentrate. Before I could think too much on that, Seth was standing next to me and adding a delicious smelling pasta concoction to my plate.

"It smells delicious," I said as I placed my napkin on my lap.

"Thanks," Seth said. "Theo, get the biscuits out of the oven, would you?"

As Theo pulled the biscuits out, I stare at Seth. "You made your own biscuits?"

He gave me a flirty grin that made my pussy tingle. "I'm an excellent biscuit maker, Libby."

They sat down with me at the island and I took a biscuit when Theo passed them to me. The food was incredible tasting and I smiled at Seth. "Theo's right. You're an amazing cook."

"Thank you," Seth said. He took a drink of beer and I tried not to drool when he licked a drop from his bottom lip.

"So, uh, how long have you guys been friends?" I asked.

"We met in high school," Theo replied.

"That's a long time."

"It is," Seth agreed.

"Have you lived together long?"

"Since we finished high school," Theo replied. "At first it was because it was cheaper to live with roommates."

"But now?"

Seth shrugged. "We enjoy each other's company."

I ate a bite of pasta and chased it down with a sip of water. "How long have you two been, um, tag teaming women?"

Libby! What the hell?

Seth and Theo both laughed and I turned bright red. "Oh God. I'm sorry. It's none of my business and I shouldn't have asked that."

"We don't mind," Theo said. "During university, I started dating a girl named Lisa. Seth and I lived in a cheap apartment together close to campus and Lisa would spend a lot of time at our place. She was attracted to Seth, I could tell, and one night when she'd had too much to drink, she proposed a threesome."

"It was her idea?" I said.

He nodded. "Yep. Honestly, it had never crossed my mind to fuck a girl with Seth before."

"Me either," Seth said.

"So that was the first night you tried it?"

Seth shook his head. "No, not that night. Lisa was drunk and we weren't taking advantage of that. We waited until she was sober and when she admitted that she still wanted it, we had the threesome."

"You weren't jealous?" I asked Theo.

He shook his head. "No. I thought maybe I would be and Seth and I talked about it beforehand but," he paused, "I wasn't. In fact, it felt…"

He trailed off and Seth took another swallow of beer before saying, "It felt right."

Theo finished the last of his pasta before wiping his mouth with a napkin. "We had sex separately a few more times after that but honestly, it was more fun together. We're both dominant and it's unbelievably hot to take a woman together."

His voice had lowered and he leaned closer as I swallowed heavily. "To have a woman impaled on both of our cocks at once, watch her moan and beg and plead to come while we're fucking her pussy and ass is incredible, Libby. It's even better if she lets us put a collar on her or restrain her."

I didn't say anything. My panties were flooded and my nipples were hard enough to cut glass, and I was afraid if I opened my mouth it would be to beg them to fuck me like that. To tie me up, collar me and make me plead for their cocks.

The idea of losing that control, to give in and let them make all the decisions was intoxicating. I had worked hard at my career, sacrificing time and energy and even relationships and it had paid off. I was a partner at only thirty-two years old. It was an incredible accomplishment and I was proud of it. But it had come at a cost, and the tight control I kept over my emotions was starting to wear thin. Wayne said my weight was the problem but there had to be more. I hadn't always been the best girlfriend and I knew that, but I tried to balance it out. I tried to make both Wayne and myself happy. Until the moment I walked in on him fucking another woman, I thought I was making it work.

Maybe I was wrong. Maybe it was the fact that I'd gained weight that had resulted in Wayne cheating on me. But what if it wasn't. Wayne wasn't dominant, not in the bedroom or out of it, and while our sex life was pleasant enough, it hadn't set the bed on fire or anything. I could try and deny it out of a sense of embarrassment or pride, but I needed men like Theo and Seth. Men who liked that I wanted to give up that control, wanted to have my hair pulled and my ass spanked and to – I bit at my bottom lip as my pussy throbbed – to wear a collar.

"You okay, Libby?" Theo asked in a low voice.

I nodded. "Yeah, sorry. I'm a little tired."

Theo reached out to touch my face before thinking better of it. "I suppose sleeping on an air mattress isn't the best way to get a good night's sleep."

I shrugged. "I'm not a great sleeper. At least not usually. Saturday night I slept like a damn baby."

I immediately blushed. Bringing up Saturday night wasn't a good idea. What the hell was I thinking?

Seth smiled at me. "Glad we could help, sweetheart."

"Why don't you sleep well, usually?" Theo asked.

"I have a hard time shutting off my brain," I said. "Saturday night though, I guess I was relaxed enough to sleep."

Theo eyed me silently before standing. "Excuse me."

He left the kitchen and I blinked at his abrupt exit as Seth stood and began to clear the island off.

"Here, let me help," I said.

"Sit and relax," Seth replied.

"No, I want to help," I insisted.

Working silently, we loaded the dishwasher. As Seth put the pan in the sink and added hot water and dish soap to it, I stared out the window over the sink. Their neighbours had their Christmas lights turned on and I watched them blink off and on. It was starting to snow and I sighed inwardly. I had upset Theo somehow and I felt terrible about it. It was best that I leave so why was I hesitating? I couldn't stay the night. That was madness.

"Libby? What's wrong, sweetheart?"

"I've made Theo angry," I said. I blinked back the hot tears that wanted to fall.

Seth shook his head before sliding his arm around my waist and pulling me up against his big, hard body. I knew I shouldn't have been encouraging his behaviour, but it felt so good to be in his arms again. "You haven't, sweetheart."

"He left so quickly," I said. "I know he's - "

"He left because he's not as good at controlling his dick as I am," Seth interrupted.

"I – what?"

"Odds are - he has a massive erection and he's probably in his bedroom yanking his crank as we speak."

I stared at him in shock. "He – he doesn't have an erection."

"Are you kidding me?" Seth said. "Sweetheart, both of us have had at least half a woody since we left your bed Sunday morning. It's only gotten worse since we discovered you were our new boss."

He gave me a rueful smile. "I don't know about Theo, but I've had to twice go to the bathroom at work and rub one out and it's only been one goddamn day since you started at the office. My dick will be rubbed raw by Friday if this keeps up."

A slightly hysterical and confused giggle dropped from my mouth. "You're lying."

"I wish I was," Seth said. "You have no idea how much we want you, Libs."

"I – I want you too," I confessed.

He groaned and before I could stop him, kissed me hard on the mouth. I returned his kiss eagerly, rubbing my body against his as he cupped my breast and squeezed.

"Libby," he whispered raggedly against my mouth, "please let us fuck you again. Please, sweetheart."

I tried to pull away when Theo said, "What's going on in here?".

Seth held me firmly and grinned at his best friend who was leaning against the door jamb. "Not much. Me just begging Libby, rather pathetically I might add, to let us fuck her again."

Theo joined us and I didn't object when he pressed up against my back. His cock was hard against my ass and I ground against him as Seth cupped my tits again.

Theo bent his head and nipped my earlobe before sliding his hand down toward my pussy. "Open your legs."

I obeyed him immediately and he groaned into my ear before cupping me through my yoga pants. "Are you wet, Libby?"

"Yes," I said.

His other hand immediately spanked me hard on the ass and I squealed as his hand tightened around my pussy. "Try again, sweet Libby."

"Yes, Sir. I'm wet, Sir," I whispered.

"Good girl," Theo said. He started to slide his hand into the waistband of my pants.

"Theo, wait."

He scowled at Seth as I whimpered in protest.

"Libby, is this what you really want?" Seth said.

"Yes," I said. "This is what I want."

"Are you sure?"

"Seth, shut up, for fuck's sake," Theo said.

"Theo, it's important," Seth snapped.

I sighed and pulled away from both of them. I crossed my arms over my torso and bit at my bottom lip. "Here's the thing – I'm going to be completely honest with you. Even though I know it's a potentially career ending move, I want to have sex with both of you. Ever since Saturday night I can't stop thinking about what it would be like to take both of you at once."

"Oh, fuck yes," Theo said before reaching for me.

I held up my hand and backed away. "But, once that happens, this has to end. You know that, right? We can't keep sleeping together."

Theo and Seth glanced at each other before Theo nodded. "If that's what you want, Libby."

"It is," I said. "After tonight, after I'm uh, fucked by both of you together, we go back to being completely professional at the office and outside of it too."

"Sweetheart, we can't fuck you together tonight," Seth said.

"Why not?"

"You've never done anal before and we need to stretch you first," Theo said bluntly.

I sighed impatiently. "I told you Saturday night that it's my body and I'm willing to give it a try. I'm sure if you go slowly and - "

"No," Seth interrupted. "We won't take the risk of hurting you, Libby."

I gave him a look of frustration. "So, I have to wait?"

"Yes," Theo said.

"Until when?" I sounded like a petulant little kid but neither Theo nor Seth seemed to notice.

Seth glanced at Theo. "What do you think? By the weekend?"

"Maybe," Theo said. "If we stretch her with a plug every night."

I blinked at them. "The weekend? It's

Tuesday! I can't wait that long."

Seth laughed. "It's only a few days, sweetheart."

"You'll come to our place every night after work and we'll get you ready for it," Theo said.

"I can't take that risk," I said. "What if someone from the office finds out?"

"They won't," Seth said. "We're very discreet with our personal lives, Libby."

"No one will find out," Theo said. "We'll give you a key to our house and you can park in the alley behind the house and come in through the back."

I bit at my lip as I considered what they were saying.

"It's this way or not at all, love," Theo said.

I sighed and wrinkled my nose at him. "Fine. But after the weekend, we end it. Do you understand?"

"Yes," Seth said.

"If you tell anyone at the office – hell, if you tell anyone at all – I'll cut off both of your sacks and nail them to my office wall for everyone to see. Deal?" I said cheerily.

They both gaped at me before Theo cleared his throat. "Yes, ma'am."

"And I'm only submissive to you in the bedroom," I said. "If you even try to be dominant at the office or - "

"We won't," Seth said. "Trust me, sweetheart. Your confidence and abilities at work are one of the sexiest things about you."

"I – really?"

He grinned as Theo said, "Yes, really."

"But you like submissive women."

"Only in the bedroom," Theo said. "We promise we won't try to pull any dominant bullshit over you at work."

I wasn't sure that I completely believed him, but my lust was overriding my common sense. I nodded. "Okay, good."

"But I can't promise that I won't occasionally look at you at work and remember how you look when you're naked, while you're wearing our collar with my dick in your mouth," Seth said.

My mouth dropped open and there was silence for a moment before I started to giggle. I shouldn't have found that funny, but God help me, I did. Seth laughed and pulled me back into his embrace. "Come on, gorgeous girl. Let's get you naked."

Chapter Five

Seth and Theo led me upstairs to Theo's bedroom.

"Why Theo's bedroom?" I asked.

"Bigger bed," Seth said with a grin. I didn't object when he started to strip off my clothes. Theo disappeared into the walk-in closet. By the time he returned, I was completely naked and Seth had my legs spread and was fingering my pussy while I clutched at his broad shoulders.

"God, Seth, you couldn't wait two minutes?"

"No," Seth said as he pumped his fingers in and out of my pussy. "Fuck, she's soaking wet already."

"Please, Sir," I moaned. "Please."

"Our little kitten is begging already," Theo said with a smug grin. "Seth, stop fingering her for a minute."

"No!" I protested and then squealed when Seth withdrew his fingers from my sopping pussy and slapped my ass hard.

"Lift her hair," Theo said as I rubbed at my

burning ass.

Theo was now naked and I stared greedily at his erect cock as he moved closer and Seth gathered my hair into a ponytail on top of my head.

"Lift your chin, Libby," Theo instructed.

I lifted my head and stared at the black leather collar he was holding in his hands. It was thinner than I thought and I eyed the silver buckle as Theo unbuckled it.

"How many other women have worn this?" I asked.

Theo glanced at Seth and I thought I saw embarrassment flicker in his eyes.

"What?" I asked.

"No one else has worn it," Theo said. "I bought it last night specifically for you."

"But you had no idea I would..."

I trailed off as Theo gave me an adorable boyish grin. "I had high hopes we could change your mind."

"Oh," I said.

There was a moment of silence and then Theo was placing the collar around my throat. He buckled it and slipped his finger between the collar and my neck before stepping back. "It looks beautiful on you, love," he said. "Show her, Seth."

Seth walked me over to the full-length mirror in the corner of the room. I stared at the collar around my throat as Theo stood to my right and Seth stood behind me.

"It looks good," I said. I wasn't lying. I never would have thought I'd say a collar looked good on me, but looking at the way the leather pressed against my pale skin made me a little hot.

Seth cupped my tits and I watched as he pulled and tugged on my nipples. It sent pleasure straight to my pussy and I moaned with need as he kissed my neck above the collar.

"Did you get the other stuff?" Seth asked Theo.

He nodded as they led me back to the bed. Sitting on the bed was a pair of leather cuffs, a bottle of lube and – I swallowed hard – a butt plug. The plug part was silver and at the opposite end a bright red jewel caught the light from the lamp.

"Give me your hands, love," Theo said.

I held them out obediently and as Seth undressed, Theo buckled the cuffs around my wrists. They were a tight fit and I stared at the metal hoops embedded in them as Seth joined us by the bed.

"Ready?" Seth asked.

"Yes," I said.

"Safe word?"

"Red."

"Good," Theo said. "Bend over the bed, spread your legs wide and hold your ass cheeks open for me, Libby."

I stared at him as my face turned bright red. I knew I would have the butt plug inserted but I thought we would make out a little first and then one of them would discreetly insert it for me. I couldn't just bend over and – and hold myself open for it. No way, no how.

"Libby," Theo prompted.

I shook my head. "No. I know I need the butt plug but I'm not going to hold myself open. That's humiliating."

"Libby," Theo said. "Do what I say. Last chance."

I shook my head and gave him a stubborn look. "No. You can make it a bit more romantic or at the very least, help me to – oh dammit!"

Seth had grabbed my arms and without a word, he turned me and bent me over the bed until my cheek was resting against the quilt and my ass was in the air. Still silent, he spanked me in a hard, quick rhythm as I squealed and twisted. I reached back and tried to protect my burning ass with my flailing hands. Seth immediately grabbed my wrists by the leather cuffs and held them against my lower back before spanking my ass again. The pain made my legs shake and I collapsed face-down on the bed and buried my face in the quilt to muffle my cries.

Seth was merciless. He spanked me at least twenty times while I wiggled and squirmed and cursed a blue streak. When I finally collapsed against the bed in silent submission, he rubbed his hand over the curve of my burning ass before pushing it between my thighs. He rubbed my shamefully wet and swollen clit as I moaned and spread my legs wide.

"On your knees, sweetheart," Seth commanded.

I climbed to my knees, keeping my face and upper body buried in the bed, and moaned when Seth pushed my thighs wide. Cool air washed over my anus, but Seth said, "Use your hands to spread yourself open, Libby."

This time I did what he asked. Certain that my face was as red as my ass, I kept my eyes squeezed shut as I reached back and held my ass cheeks apart. I was embarrassed beyond belief but there was also a deep and painfully strong part of me that was incredibly turned on by what they were forcing me to do.

I moaned and twitched when Theo sat down on the bed beside me and ran his rough fingers over my clit. He used the moisture from my pussy and rubbed his fingers over my anus as my fingers dug into my butt cheeks.

I gasped when Seth pressed a kiss against my right ass cheek. "You look so pretty in this position, Libby."

"Yeah, right," I muttered.

I received a hard spank to my left cheek from Theo for my impertinence and I gasped and cried out, "I'm sorry, Sir."

Theo rubbed my aching ass. "Hold still, love."

The lube was cold against my ass and I tried to clench my ass shut when Theo probed at me with his slick finger.

"No," Seth said. "Don't do that, sweetheart. Relax."

"Easy for you to say," I added a hasty "Sir" before he could spank me.

I could hear the grin in Seth's voice as he said, "Take some deep breaths."

I breathed deep and tried not to moan when Theo eased his finger past the tight ring of muscle. "How does that feel?"

"Like I have a finger up my ass?" I said.

Both men laughed and my answering giggle turned to a moan of need when Seth rubbed my clit.

My discomfort disappeared in an instant and I rubbed my pussy against Seth's fingers as I dropped my hands to the bed.

"Make her come first," Theo murmured.

I cried out when both men leaned over me and kissed their way up my back. The combination of their mouths and tongue, the feel of Seth's rough fingers against my swollen clit and the way Theo trailed his free hand up and down the back of my thigh, brought my climax on in an embarrassingly quick fashion. I moaned and shuddered and clawed at the quilt as Seth kissed my shoulder before brushing my hair back from my sweaty face.

"Hold your ass open again, sweetheart," he demanded.

My embarrassment gone, I did what he asked, spreading my cheeks wide as Theo removed his finger. I jerked when he added more lube and Seth kissed my back again. Thanks to my orgasm, I was more relaxed than before, but I still tensed the moment I felt the blunt end of the plug against my ass.

"Don't tense," Theo said.

"I'm not."

He slapped the back of my thigh and I grunted in pain before saying, "I'm trying not to, Sir."

My fingers squeezed my sore ass as Theo said, "Take a deep breath and push back against the plug."

I did what he said, groaning a little at the pressure as he steadily pushed it into my ass. There was a brief eye-watering burst of pain and then nothing but a feeling of dull pressure in my butt.

"You okay?" Seth asked.

"Yes, Sir," I replied. "Is it in?"

"It is." Theo leaned over and pressed a kiss against my cheek. "You did so well, love. How do you feel?"

"Very glad that you ignored my suggestion to just stick your dick in my ass," I said.

They both laughed and I made a small noise of protest when Theo took my arms and lifted me to my knees.

"Off the bed, Libby," he said.

"What? No, why?" I didn't even want to try and walk with the plug.

"Because we want to show you how pretty your ass is," Seth said.

I tried to resist when they pulled me off the bed, but I was no match for their strength. I felt incredibly self-conscious as they walked me over to the mirror. Afraid the plug would fall out, I kept clenching my ass around it and I was shocked at the little spikes of pleasure it sent through my body.

They turned me away from the mirror and I stared at the wall as Theo said, "Turn your head and look, Libby."

"I'd rather not," I said.

He started to bend me over and I hastily turned my head. "No, wait. I'll look, Sir. I'll look!"

I stared over my shoulder at my flaming red ass and the jewel between my ass cheeks. The red of the jewel matched the skin on my butt and I twitched when Seth ran his fingers over one ass cheek.

"So pretty, sweetheart."

I moaned a little when Theo pressed on the jewelled part. He grinned at Seth and my cheeks flushed. I knew some women got pleasure from having something shoved in their ass, but I didn't think I would be one of them.

"Our little kitten looks so pretty in her collar, maybe we should get a tail for her too," Theo said thoughtfully as he stared at my ass in the mirror.

My eyes widened and I shook my head immediately. "No fucking way, Theo. I am not having a tail hanging out of my ass."

Theo grinned at Seth. "Sounds like pet play is a hard limit."

"Damn straight it is," I said. "You come anywhere near me with a tail and I'll scream red so loudly, your neighbours will hear it."

Theo leaned forward and pressed a kiss against my mouth. "Understood, love. Come back to the bed."

We returned to the bed. Seth cupped one breast and toyed with my nipple as Theo sat on the bed before reclining on his back. I was shaking my head before the words were out of his mouth.

"I'm not riding you," I snapped. I could hear the anxiety and shame in my voice.

Seth rubbed my lower back as Theo said, "I don't want you to ride me, love. I want you to sit on my face."

My jaw dropped and I pulled away from Seth. "You what?"

"I want to taste my kitten's sweet cunt," Theo said.

"No."

"It'll be fine, Libby," Seth said. He tried to guide me closer to the bed and I tore away from him. Adrenaline was rushing through my veins and Theo sat up and gave me a look of concern.

"Love, it's okay."

"It's not," I said. "I'm-I'm yellow right now and if you try and make me do this, I'll be red. Do you understand? It all stops, and I won't come back to your place."

"We understand," Seth said immediately.

"We'll do a different position," Theo said. "It's okay, love."

I stared wide-eyed at them before whispering, "I'm sorry."

"Don't be," Theo said. He crossed to me and took me into his embrace, pressing kisses against my face and my mouth. "Don't ever apologize for telling us exactly how you feel. That's why we have a safe word, right?"

"Right," I said shakily.

"Do you want to stop, sweetheart?" Seth had joined us and he gave me a solemn look.

"No," I said. "No, I don't want to stop."

Theo and Seth glanced at each other and I shook my head. "I'm good now. Just – I don't want to sit on your face."

"Okay," Theo said before giving me another gentle kiss.

He led me back to the bed and I didn't protest when he and Seth had me sit at the head of the bed with my back leaning against the headboard, my knees bent and my feet resting on the bed. There was added pressure on the plug and I shifted a bit as

Theo pushed my thighs apart before stretching out between them. He kissed the patch of curls on my pussy as Seth kneeled next to me. One hard hand was stroking his cock and I stared at the bead of pre-cum at the tip of it before leaning down and licking it away.

"Fuck!" Seth muttered. He cupped the back of my head and I sucked at his cock with enthusiasm as Theo licked my inner thighs. I moaned around Seth's cock when Theo kissed the wet lips of my pussy. When his tongue wandered over my clit, I arched my hips and clutched at his head as I stared up at Seth.

He gathered up my hair and pulled roughly on it. "Suck harder, Libby."

I tried to concentrate on Seth's dick, but Theo's tongue was goddamn magic. It didn't take long before I was moaning and thrusting my hips against Theo's face. I pulled Theo's hair with one hand and stroked the base of Seth's cock with the other as he pushed his dick in and out of my mouth.

I was already close to a second orgasm. When Theo reached under me and wiggled the plug in my ass, my climax was hot and immediate and lasted incredibly long. Wave after wave of intense pleasure flooded my lower body. My scream was muffled by Seth's cock and he shoved it in deep as I writhed against Theo's tongue and lips.

Seth pulled out and I gasped in some much-needed oxygen as I pushed at Theo's head. I was shaking all over and was so weak I slumped against the headboard. I barely noticed when Theo sat up and rolled a condom onto his dick before lying on his back next to me.

Seth was urging me to my knees and I pouted and whined, "Tired, Sir."

"I know, sweetheart. Theo's going to fuck you and then you can sleep."

I smiled at the thought of being fucked as Seth pulled on my right thigh. "Come on, sweetheart. Leg over Theo, now."

Feeling almost drunk from my unbelievable orgasm, I did what he asked. It wasn't until I was straddling Theo, my knees pressed against his hips as Seth pulled my arms behind my back and held them firmly, that I realized what was happening.

Theo was beginning to press his dick against my opening and I froze as fresh adrenaline pumped through my veins.

"I can't be on top!" I shouted like an idiot. "Stop, wait, I'm going to hurt...oh fuck!"

Seth had pushed me down, impaling me on Theo's thick cock. I moaned and wiggled and tried to ignore how good it felt to have my pussy filled to the brim with dick.

"Stop," I whispered unconvincingly. "Theo, I'm too heavy."

"You're not," he rasped as he reached up and cupped my tits. He pulled hard on the nipples and I arched my back. "Baby, your soft curves feel like heaven. I need you to fuck me right now before I go insane."

"Are you sure?" I whispered as Seth tightened his hold on my arms.

"Fuck, yes," Theo groaned. "Seth, let her go."

He released my arms and Theo tugged me down

until I was bent over him with my hands resting on the bed above his shoulders. He kissed my upper chest and I rubbed my nipples against his chest as his hands cupped my tender ass. He thrust in and out and I moaned with pleasure before bouncing enthusiastically on his dick.

"Fuck," he muttered again, "the plug makes her even tighter."

"Libby, look at me."

I turned my head and automatically opened my mouth for Seth's cock. He was kneeling next to my head again and I sucked on his cock as Theo fucked me hard. His rhythm was rough and out-of-control and I cried out when one of his hands pushed on the plug in my ass and the other rubbed furiously at my clit.

Seth held tightly to my hair, guiding my mouth back and forth over his dick as Theo made another hoarse groan. "Fuck, I'm not going to... I can't..."

His body arched beneath mine and he pinched my clit hard. It should have hurt, and it did, but the pain brought on a third and completely unexpected orgasm. I forgot completely about hurting Theo and ground my pelvis against his as he grabbed my hips and came deep inside of me. Seth pulled me away from his cock and into a sitting position with a hard tug to my collar. He pumped his dick with his hand and came with a loud roar of pleasure, his cum splattering all over my breasts.

Panting harshly, Theo helped me ease off of him. I fell to the bed on my side, my entire body quivering and pulsing. Theo disposed of the condom as Seth used a towel to wipe my chest clean. I kept my eyes closed and moaned happily when both men slid into the bed on either side of me. Seth was at my back and I jerked when he touched the plug still in my ass.

"Take it out," I whispered.

"No, sweetheart," he said.

"Please, Sir?" I asked.

"No," Seth repeated.

I must have been pouting because Theo made a low chuckle before pressing a kiss against my mouth. "The longer you wear it, the sooner you can take Seth's dick in your ass."

"But it's getting late and I should go home."

"No," Seth said. "You're spending the night with us, Libby."

I should have argued. I should have gotten up, taken the plug out of my damn ass, dressed and driven home. Instead, I snuggled in closer to their hard bodies and sighed with pleasure when Theo cupped my breast and Seth kissed my back.

"Sleep now, Libby."

"Yes, Sir," I murmured.

Chapter Six

"Libby?" Mario knocked on my office door. "Why are you still here? The office closes at five thirty, or did we forget to tell you that?"

He grinned good-naturedly at me and I laughed. "I wanted to finish up a few things."

"Ah, well since you're still here, can I take a few minutes of your time?"

"Of course," I said as I leaned back in my chair. "What's up?"

"Did anyone go over the Christmas office schedule with you?" He asked as he sat in the chair across from my desk.

"Sandra sent me the email," I replied. "I told her I would be more than happy to be the partner at the office between Christmas and New Year's."

"She mentioned that," Mario said. "But I talked to Jeff and Emmett and we've made the decision to close the office completely."

"Oh," I said.

"We'll have a couple of the support staff come in for a few hours each day between the 27th and the

2nd, and Jim has offered to be on call if anything should come up."

"As the newest associate partner, shouldn't I be the one to get the 'work during the holidays' job instead of Jim?" I asked with a small smile.

Mario laughed. "We don't want to scare you into quitting your first month."

"I don't mind working," I said. I didn't. I hadn't been here long enough to make any friends so the prospect of having a week off with nothing to do wasn't exactly appealing.

Maybe you could spend it with Seth and Theo.

I ignored my inner voice. Seth and Theo would have holiday plans with their families. I wasn't asking them to spend Christmas with me. That was ridiculous. Christmas was Tuesday and after this weekend I wouldn't even be seeing them outside of work anymore.

"Libby?"

"Sorry, what was that?" I apologized.

"I asked if you were going home for the holidays?"

"No, which is why I can work."

"We're going to keep you busy enough after the holidays," Mario said with a laugh. "Enjoy your free time while you still have it. Sandra has sent out the email to our clients with our holiday office hours. I asked her to add Etco Drilling Ltd. to the email so that Charles knows.

"Perfect, thanks," I said. Not that it mattered. Charles had my personal cell number and wouldn't hesitate to call it if he couldn't get a hold of me at the office.

"You bet." Mario glanced at his watch. "It's almost seven now. You should get out of here."

"I'm about to head home," I lied.

"Good. See you tomorrow."

"Bye, Mario."

He walked out of my office and I packed up my laptop and shut off the lights to my office before heading to the elevator. I was going to Seth and Theo's place for sex, butt stretching and if I was lucky, multiple orgasms.

I shivered all over as I walked to my car. My ass was sore, more from being spanked than the plug, not to mention my thighs ached. Hell, all of my muscles ached but it wasn't stopping me from going back to them. Fucking two men I worked with was a mind-numbingly stupid idea, but I was addicted to what they did and said to me.

What happens when they blackmail you over this? When they demand better pay and bigger clients or they'll tell the other partners what you let them do to you?

I ignored my inner voice. They wouldn't blackmail me. I didn't know them very well and maybe it was stupid to go with my gut on this one, but I knew instinctively that blackmailing me or using this brief affair to get them ahead at the office wasn't their style. Trying to convince me to keep fucking them though, was an entirely different story.

I climbed into my car and threw my purse on the seat beside me. The thought of allowing Seth and Theo to convince me to keep going with our affair was intoxicating. What if I liked fucking both of them at once? It hardly seemed fair to try it and then never get to do it again.

I started my car. One, I couldn't keep fucking them and two, I was being presumptuous. Just because Seth and Theo were willing to help me live my fantasy of fucking two men at once, didn't mean they were willing to keep going once we actually fucked.

You got that right. You're too fat to keep them interested. You know that, don't you, Libby? In fact, I'm pretty sure they're throwing you a pity fuck. Men who look like them are not chubby chasers.

My stomach rolled with nausea and I forced deep breaths of cold air into my lungs. They weren't throwing me a pity fuck. They thought I was gorgeous and sexy and they loved my curves. Just because inner me had suddenly turned into a stone-cold bitch who apparently reveled in making me feel bad, it didn't mean I had to listen to her. They didn't believe I was fat. Hell, Theo had even let me ride him and he was fine afterwards.

Are you sure? You didn't see him get up and move around, did you? He was still in bed when you left this morning. You didn't even see him at the office today. Maybe he didn't come in. Maybe he's at the hospital getting those crushed ribs checked out. You didn't even think about your goddamn weight, did you? You rode him like the world's fattest cowgirl and he had a prime viewing of every single part of you that jiggles. Of your fat rolls and the way your tits sag. I bet you crushed his need for you and his ribs in one single –

"Shut up!" I snapped out loud. "They still want me. Would they have asked me to come over tonight if they didn't?"

My inner self had nothing to say to that. I tried to will my nausea away. I had planned on stopping and grabbing a bite to eat but the nausea had driven away my appetite. Instead, I drove directly toward Seth and Theo's house. It was fine. Everything was fine. Theo and Seth wanted me. They thought I was beautiful. They wanted me, and I was going to let them have me.

ॐ ॐ

"Libby," Seth smiled at me when I stuck my head into the kitchen. I had used the key he gave me this morning to let myself into the back door after parking a street over and walking down the alley. "How are you?"

"Good," I said. He took my jacket and disappeared down the front hallway. When he returned, he pressed a warm kiss against my mouth and squeezed my ass. I winced and a wicked little grin crossed his face. "Sore bottom?"

"Yes," I replied.

"I guess you'd better be a good girl tonight then," Seth said with another wicked smile.

"Sure," I said absently. I yelped when Seth gave me a hard slap to the ass.

"Misbehaving already," he said.

"I'm not!"

"You are. You're distracted and unfocused which means you're thinking about work. You don't think about work when you're here, sweetheart."

"I'm not thinking about work," I protested.

"No?" Seth raised his eyebrows. "Then what are you thinking about?"

I worried my bottom lip with my teeth. "Where's Theo?"

"He had an errand to run," Seth said. "He'll be back soon."

"Is he, I mean, does he feel okay?" I asked.

Seth gave me a puzzled look. "What do you mean?"

Oh God, he was going to make me say it. My cheeks burning, I said, "Is he sore or, ah, injured?"

"Why would he be injured?" Seth was looking at me like I had grown two heads, but I was positive he was being deliberately obtuse. Anger flared in me and I scowled at him.

"Because I'm heavy and you two assholes made me ride him last night!" My nausea grew, and I felt frantic and angry and out of control. I shouted foolishly, "I told you I didn't want to be on top and now Theo probably has crushed ribs and you're being too polite to tell me!"

I yelped again when Seth turned me and pushed me over the island. He held me down with one hand in the middle of my back as his other hand shoved up my skirt. I was wearing thick tights and he yanked them down to my knees, dragging my underwear down with them.

Without saying a word, he spanked my already-sore ass with heavy slaps. It burned like fire and I immediately began to cry and plead for him to stop. He ignored me, and I slumped across the table as his rough hand kept up a steady rhythm of spanks.

Within minutes, my anger and fear had left and despite how much it hurt, a weird kind of peace consumed me. I pressed my hot cheek against the cool marble as I accepted the spanking. I floated happily in the bubble, still feeling the stinging pain of each of Seth's spanks but the pain was tinged with sweetness and pleasure.

I hadn't realized it, but all day long I'd been stressed and overwhelmed. My desire to do well at my new job and prove I was worthy of partnership, my fear that I had hurt Theo, even my hard-to-shake belief that Seth and Theo weren't actually attracted to me had weighed on me. But for the first time, I wasn't worried about proving myself at my job, or stressed about my looks or even feeling shame for possibly hurting Theo. I couldn't be. Right or wrong, Seth's firm discipline of my outburst had sent me to my happy place and I felt…free.

"Spanking already?"

I was only vaguely aware of Theo's deep voice, but I whined a little when Seth stopped spanking me and ran his hand over my ass.

"She was being disrespectful and raising her voice," Seth said.

"Why?" Theo asked.

"She has this silly idea that she hurt you when you were fucking her last night." Seth's voice was dark with disapproval, but I didn't notice. I was still floating.

"Are you kidding me?" Theo forced me to straighten up from the table. He smelled like snow and pine trees and I inhaled deeply as he studied me. "Christ, is she in subspace?"

"She can't be," Seth said as he turned me to face him. "She can't possibly trust us enough yet to…"

He trailed off and I smiled dreamily at him.

"Sweetheart, you okay?"

"Yes, Sir," I said. "Can I please come now?"

My peaceful, dreamy state was already starting to subside, and I caught the look between Theo and Seth. "What?"

"Nothing, love," Theo said. "Come to the bedroom."

He peeled off my tights and underwear as Seth pulled my skirt down over my ass. Theo took my hand and I followed him to his bedroom. I wanted to stay in that dreamy floating state forever but by the time I was standing in front of his bed, it was gone completely. The frustration was almost overwhelming, and I blinked back the hot tears. What the hell was wrong with me? I would not cry in front of Seth and Theo. I was their goddamn boss and I wouldn't fucking cry in front of them.

Are you kidding me? You let them put a collar around your neck and a plug up your ass. You call them both Sir and suck their dicks until your jaw aches, but you won't cry in front of them?

No, I fucking well wouldn't.

"You all right, sweetheart?"

"Fine," I snapped irritably at Seth. I immediately tensed and fought my urge to cover my ass with my hands. My attitude almost guaranteed a punishment.

To my utter surprise, Seth simply started to undress me while Theo went to the closet. I was naked when he returned and he buckled the collar around my neck and the leather cuffs around my wrists before Seth urged me onto the bed. I was still incredibly close to tears, my skin felt too tight and hot and that lovely feeling I had earlier was a distant memory.

Be a bad girl. They'll spank you again and you can get it back.

Now that was a very fucking good idea. I suddenly didn't care that my ass was swollen and painful or that the faint bruises I had from yesterday would become dark purple blotches by tomorrow. I needed that feeling back. I needed it and they were going to give it to me.

I moved my legs restlessly on the bed as Seth and Theo, still fully-clothed, laid down on either side of me. I glared at Theo. "Not going to get naked because you don't want me to see the bruises on your ribs?"

He arched his eyebrows at me. "Why would I have bruises?"

"Because a fat girl rode you last night?" I retorted.

Seth immediately rolled me to my side to face Theo and I could have crowed with victory even as I was tensing for that first painful slap. Instead of a spank, he kissed my upper back as Theo cupped my breast and toyed with my nipple.

"No," I whined. "No, not that."

Oh my God, what the hell was wrong with me? I was acting like a spoiled brat.

"Yes, this," Theo said.

"I'm being bad," I moaned and arched my back

as Seth licked my spine and Theo pulled on my nipple. "I need to be punished."

"No, Libby," Seth said. His hands traced circles on the back of my thighs as he kissed the top of my shoulder.

"Theo, please," I whimpered. "Please spank me, Sir."

"No, you've had enough spanking for now," Theo said. He kissed me hard on the mouth, forcing my lips open so he could thrust his tongue between them. I sucked at it before fisting my hands in his shirt and clinging to him. He tasted so damn good and as desire and need burned in my belly, I could feel my frustration melting away.

Seth was lifting my leg and hooking it behind his. He was wearing jeans and the denim made my ass sting, but I rubbed my butt against the bulge of his erection anyway. As Theo trailed his fingers down across my belly, I whispered, "Please, Sir."

I realized with sudden clarity that I didn't want to be teased or tormented. If I couldn't have that floaty feeling back, I wanted an orgasm. Wanted and needed it in a way I didn't quite understand.

"Don't tease," I moaned. "Please, don't tease."

"No teasing this time, baby," Theo whispered into my ear before nipping my earlobe. "We know what you need."

As Seth reached around and cupped my breast, Theo slipped his hand between my legs. His warm fingers found my swollen clit and he rubbed it with precise strokes that had me on the edge almost immediately. I cried out when Seth pinched my nipple hard as his other hand pulled on my collar and forced my head back. I arched my body, rubbing my ass against Seth's erection as Theo stroked my clit.

I moaned – or maybe I screamed – both their names as my climax rushed over me and I collapsed in a quivering heap between them. As the high of my orgasm started to fade, I slumped against Theo and tried to bury my face in his t-shirt, but Seth tugged on my collar and forced my head back.

"Is she in subspace again?" He asked.

Theo studied my face before shaking his head. "No, but she is more relaxed now."

"Good," Seth said.

I tried to hide my surprise when both men moved in close and cuddled me. Theo stroked my hair and Seth rubbed my thigh and hip as I stared up at Theo.

"Do you feel okay, love?"

"Yes. Why aren't you fucking me? Did I hurt you yesterday?" I asked anxiously.

He scowled and tucked my hair back behind my ear. "No, you most definitely didn't hurt me. Also, if I ever hear you refer to yourself as a fat girl again, I'll spank you until you can't sit down. Do you understand?"

I nodded, stupidly happy at the thought of being punished by Theo. "Then why aren't we fucking?"

"Later," Theo said.

I leaned my head back until it was resting against Seth's chest. He pressed a kiss against my temple. "How do you feel, Libby?"

I frowned. Why did they keep asking me that?

"Fine." I hesitated and then said, "What's

subspace?"

"Subspace is a reaction to intense stimuli," Seth said. "It varies for each submissive but, generally speaking, it's an awareness change. Lots of subs refer to it as flying or floating."

I jerked against him. "That – it felt like that for me earlier when you were spanking me."

He cupped my breast and squeezed it gently as Theo said, "When a submissive goes into subspace, his or her Dom needs to be very careful."

"Why?" I asked.

"Because usually a submissive doesn't care what happens to them at that point. They're completely unaware and will let a scene go too long. They can be hurt if the Dom doesn't know what he or she is doing."

I shivered and Seth gave my breast another almost soothing squeeze. "That rarely happens, sweetheart. A submissive takes a long time to go into subspace with a new Dom. She needs to feel complete trust with her Dom before she goes into subspace around them. By the time she does, her Dom knows her limits intimately and won't let a scene go too far, even if his sub isn't safe wording."

"Oh," I said. "But you said I was in subspace earlier and we've barely, uh, played together."

Theo and Seth glanced at each other and I groaned in sudden understanding. "Oh my God, so I'm not just a freak, I'm a super freak."

"You're not a freak," Theo scolded. "Being submissive doesn't make you a freak, Libs."

"No, but going into subspace so quickly does," I argued.

"It's a bit unusual," Seth admitted, "but you didn't go in very deep and you didn't stay in it very long."

"I was upset and frustrated when I wasn't, uh, in subspace anymore," I said. "It's why I begged you to spank me."

I turned bright red and buried my face against Theo's chest. I smelled pine trees again as I said, "I am a freak."

"You're not," Seth insisted. "There can be a low coming out of subspace – it's normal. Besides, going into subspace so quickly with me was a gift of trust and I'm glad it happened."

I sighed and said, "I was feeling stressed and worried and when you started spanking me, even though it hurt, it made all of that fade away. Maybe because it hurt and that was all I could concentrate on, you know?"

"Were you spanked in your previous relationships?" Theo asked.

"No," I said. "The thought of being spanked and of being forced to, you know, suck on a dick or even being, um, fucked when it wasn't exactly, uh…"

Oh God, how did I say this without really sounding like a freak?

"When it wasn't one hundred percent clear that you wanted to be fucked?" Seth asked.

I nodded, my cheeks burning like fire and my entire body tense. "Yeah. Anyway, those things turned me on and I knew that they did, but my previous partners weren't like you and I was shy and nervous about certain things. Sometimes when

I was having sex, I would close my eyes and pretend they were forcing me to have sex with them. It always made it hotter, but I'd feel so dirty after. Like I had used them for something they would never understand and would be disgusted by if they knew."

I took a deep breath. "My ex, Wayne, he was – was not experimental at all. I had more self-confidence when I started dating him and I asked him one night to pin my arms above my head while we were having sex in missionary style. He would only do two positions – me on top and missionary. I never even tried doggy style until that night in the hotel room with the two of you."

"Christ," Theo said in a low mutter.

Libby! Stop talking! You do not have to spill every single humiliating detail.

Inner me was right but I couldn't seem to stop. There was a cathartic release in telling them.

"Anyway, he did it and it was hot to be pinned down so I asked him a few times to do that. He always would but it started to lose some of its appeal. I guess because it never truly felt real. Like I knew if I actually tried to break free, he'd let me and that wasn't what I wanted. I wanted to be...helpless. You know?"

"Yes," Seth said. He kissed the back of my shoulder as his fingers stroked across my nipple.

"I thought about asking him to restrain me to the bed with handcuffs or ropes, but I couldn't work up the nerve. But I asked him to spank me once. I'd had a couple glasses of wine and figured it wouldn't hurt to ask, right? Only, the look he gave me was so humiliating. He couldn't even hide how disgusted he was by the idea. He said no immediately, and I tried to pass it off as a joke. In the morning, he wanted to know why I would ever ask him to hurt me like that and I – I told him I had more wine than he thought and was really drunk."

Theo leaned forward and kissed my forehead. "I'm sorry, Libs."

"It's fine," I said. "It's not a big deal. But it's why I reacted the way I did when you guys threatened to spank me at the bar that night. My biggest fantasy was just handed to me on a silver platter."

"I'm glad we could help," Seth murmured into my ear. His fingers pulled on my nipple and I made a soft moan.

"Are you – are you sure that I'm not a freak for wanting to be hurt?" I asked.

"Positive," Theo said. "Why did you and Wayne break up?"

I immediately tensed and Seth kissed my shoulder again as Theo rubbed my hip. "Tell us the truth, sweetheart."

I didn't want to, but fuck I'd already spilled my pathetic sex experience to them. Why not go for the gold, right?

"When I first started dating Wayne I was thin," I said. "I had lost a lot of weight, but it took work to stay that way. I was never happy constantly watching what I ate and going to the gym for two hours a day. My career was going well and I was busy with that. Eventually I stopped counting calories and, instead, tried to eat healthy and do some exercising every day. For some people, that's enough. It isn't for me, and I gained the weight back until I was my normal size."

Theo and Seth didn't reply and I said hastily, "I'm very healthy. My blood pressure is good and my cholesterol level is completely normal and - "

"Libs, stop," Seth said. "Your health is your own business, not ours. We're not judging you for anything."

I blinked at him in surprise before continuing. "Right. Well, anyway, Wayne didn't seem to be bothered by my weight gain. We still had sex and he never called me fat or anything. But then we started having sex less and less. I blamed it on how busy I was with building my career, and Wayne was, well, he was pretending to try and open his own restaurant. I never even thought it was because of my weight gain. Then I came home early from work one day and found Wayne banging a younger and thinner woman in our bed."

"Asshole!" Theo snapped as Seth made a sound of disgust.

"I broke it off with him, obviously, but I asked him why he cheated. I thought he would say because I spent so much time and energy on my career." I laughed bitterly. "I couldn't have been more wrong. He said it was my weight. He said that he was tired of being that guy with his friends – the guy who had a fat girlfriend and all his buddies felt sorry for him and were secretly glad it wasn't them. He also said that I…"

I trailed off and Seth rubbed my back. "Tell us, sweetheart."

"He said that I was so fat it hurt him when we had sex and I was on top," I said. "He said that he had a cracked rib from letting me ride him."

"He was lying," Theo said.

"He went to the doctor," I replied.

"I don't fucking care if he went to the doctor or if he did have a cracked rib," Theo snapped. "He didn't get it from you riding him."

"Fuck," Seth muttered, "so, that's why you freaked out about sitting on Theo's face and about being on top."

"I don't want to hurt you like I hurt Wayne," I said. "It's humiliating and - "

"He was lying," Theo repeated.

"He wasn't as big as you are," I said. "He was taller than me, but I probably weigh more than him now and - "

Theo cupped my face, his fingers digging into my cheek as he forced my head up to look him in the eye. "Look at me, Libby. You are not too heavy to ride a man's dick, and you're going to ride both Seth and me repeatedly until you believe it."

"I don't want to," I said.

Theo gave me a predatory grin that both unnerved me and lit up my nerve endings with lust. "You don't get a say in the matter, love. You belong to us and we'll fuck you however and in whatever position we want. Is that clear?"

I swallowed and licked my lips. "Theo, I don't - "

"Is that clear?" He repeated.

"Yes, Sir," I whispered.

"Good." He bent his head and sucked my right

nipple into his mouth. He bit it hard and I cried out, my back arching as Seth pulled my legs apart and pushed his hand between them. He cupped my pussy, rubbing it almost angrily as Theo licked away the sting of his bite.

"Seth," he said, "I want to use the clamps on her tonight."

"Fuck, yes," Seth said. "Get her nipples nice and hard while I grab them from the - "

I blushed furiously when he was interrupted by the loud growling of my stomach.

"Sorry," I said.

"Did you eat dinner?" Seth asked with a frown.

I shook my head. "No, I worked late and then I wasn't hungry. I'll have a bigger breakfast in the morning."

"No," Seth said. "You need to eat, Libs."

"I don't." I rubbed the bulge at the front of Theo's jeans. He groaned and Seth gave him a warning look.

"Hey," I said when both men pulled away from me, "I don't want to stop."

"Not your decision, remember, love?" Theo said with a wicked grin. "Besides, I should go and grab the tree. It's still strapped to the top of the car."

I gave him a blank look as Seth said, "On your hands and knees, sweetheart."

My stomach made a happy little flip of excitement. Seth had changed his mind and even though I was hungry, I wanted his dick a whole fucking lot more than food. I climbed to my hands and knees and spread my legs eagerly when Seth pushed up behind me.

"Good girl," he praised. "Spread your ass cheeks for me."

I gave him a startled look, my gaze dropping to the plug he held in his right hand. "What?"

"Spread your cheeks, sweetheart." He tapped my burning ass with the end of the plug. "We'll pop this in and then I'll make you something to eat."

"You're going to make me wear the plug while I'm eating?"

"Yes," he said. "Now, take a deep breath and try to relax. This one is a bigger size than yesterday's plug."

"Fuck," I muttered but I grabbed my ass cheeks and spread them apart as Seth spread lube over my anus and the plug.

"Ready, sweetheart?" He asked.

"Is anyone ever ready to have a plug stuck in their ass?" I asked.

He laughed and kissed my lower back. "You're my good girl, Libs. Relax, please."

I tingled with happiness when he called me his good girl and buried my face into the quilt as Seth eased the plug into my ass.

"Oh my God," I moaned.

Theo reached under me and pinched my nipples hard. The sharp pain distracted me from the dull pain in my ass and I gasped and tried to wiggle away. He slapped my dangling breast and wound his hand in my hair, yanking my face up until I was staring at him.

"Be good, Libby," he warned as Seth pushed the

plug in deeper.

"I – I am, Sir," I gasped.

"There, how does that feel?" Seth asked as he patted my ass cheek.

"Uh, good, I think," I said. He pushed on the plug at the same time Theo pulled on one nipple and I cried out like a needy cat. "Oh please, I'm not hungry. Please!"

"Liar," Seth said and gave my throbbing ass a hard slap. "Let's go to the kitchen, sweetheart."

Theo helped me off the bed but shook his head when I reached for my clothes. "You don't need them."

I balked immediately. "I can't walk around naked."

"Why not?" Seth asked. "The blinds are all closed. No one to see you but us."

"I can't," I repeated. "I don't want to safe word so please don't make me go naked."

Seth nodded and stripped off his shirt. "You can wear this but no bra or panties. Clear?"

"Yes, Sir. Thank you, Sir," I said gratefully. I tugged his t-shirt over my head. I was afraid it would be too small, but it was actually too big and fell to mid-thigh. I felt much better even though the plug in my ass made it feel weird to walk and it would be even harder to sit.

"Ready?" Seth asked.

"Yes, Sir," I replied.

He took my hand and I followed him and Theo out of the bedroom.

Chapter Seven

"Do you have any idea how hard it is to hang balls when you're doing that?" I said.

Theo laughed and squeezed my tits again, rubbing his crotch against my ass as I stood on my tiptoes to hang the round silver ornament on one of the branches. His movement jostled the plug in my ass and I couldn't help but moan.

"Someone's getting horny," he said.

"I've been horny since I got here," I replied. "But someone made me eat dinner first and then someone else made me decorate their Christmas tree."

"Hey, it can't be sex, sex, sex all the time," Seth said as he crawled out from under the tree. "We're not just dicks for your pleasure, you filthy girl."

"Really?" I said. Theo was kissing my neck and I arched into his hands when he cupped my breasts again and played with my nipples through the fabric of Seth's t-shirt.

"Mostly," Seth said as he watched my nipples harden under Theo's ministration. "Fuck, are we done decorating this goddamn tree yet?"

"Yes," Theo said. "Did you plug the lights in?"

Seth nodded and brushed some pine needles from his shoulders. "Yeah, turn them on."

Theo flicked the switch to turn on the lights. The Christmas lights flickered to life and Seth joined us as we stared up at the glowing tree.

"It's beautiful," I said.

"Yes, beautiful," Seth replied. He was staring at me and I gave him a sweet smile as he took my hand and kissed my knuckles.

While Seth made me dinner, Theo had set the tree up in their living room. I was secretly thrilled when they asked me to help decorate it. I knew it was stupid. I was only here to have sex with them, but even naked under Seth's shirt and wearing a plug in my ass, it had felt good to do something with them that wasn't sex related.

Be careful, Libby. You're thinking dangerous thoughts. This isn't a relationship and it all ends the minute they both get their dicks into you at the same time.

I know, I thought irritably to inner me. *I know, so give it a rest, would you?*

"Libby?"

"Sorry, what was that?" I smiled apologetically at Theo.

"I said it was getting late," he replied.

I glanced at the clock over the fireplace. It was almost ten and all of us had to work in the morning. I ignored my disappointment. Yes, I had loved decorating the tree with them and drinking hot chocolate and laughing and swapping childhood

Christmas stories like we were in some kind of weird threesome relationship. But apparently, deep down, I was more interested in the sex. Pathetic, but true. I would have happily given up all of that if I'd known it meant I wouldn't get laid tonight. Ignoring how sorry I felt for myself, I smiled cheerfully at them. "Yes, it is. Thank you for dinner. I had a lovely time. Should I leave the plug in for a few more hours and then bring it, um, back to you tomorrow night?"

"What are you talking about?" Seth asked with a frown.

"The butt plug," I said patiently. "Should I take it out now and leave it here or drive home with it in and take it out in another hour or so?"

"You're not going home," Theo said. "You're marching your sweet little ass up to the bedroom so we can fuck you."

Excitement radiated through me but I said, "I know its late and we have work in the morning so - "

"Libby," Seth warned, "if you keep arguing with us, you will get spanked again."

I shut my mouth with a snap and took Theo's offered hand as Seth shut the lights off on the Christmas tree. We walked upstairs to Theo's bedroom and Seth disappeared into the closet as Theo stripped off my shirt before stepping behind me. He was rubbing my clit with one hand and wiggling the plug in my ass with the other when Seth returned. I was moaning and rubbing my pussy against Theo's hand and paid no attention to what Seth was carrying.

When he bent and sucked on my right nipple, I wound my fingers through his thick hair and held him tightly. He sucked and licked until my nipple was hard and swollen.

Theo stopped playing with the plug in my ass and said, "Put your arms behind your back, love."

I did what he asked, a little thrill going through me when he hooked his arm around both of mine and held me firmly. I was trapped against him and I arched my back, pushing more of my breast into Seth's mouth as Theo bent his head and kissed me.

The pain on my nipple had me yanking my mouth from Theo's. I hissed and stared at the small metal alligator clamp fastened to my right nipple. It had a silver chain attached to it and I moaned and tried to wiggle free when Seth adjusted the fit.

"Too tight!" I gasped.

"It isn't," Seth said.

"It hurts!"

"It's supposed to," he said with a small grin. He sucked on my left nipple and I tried to will it not to harden so he couldn't attach the clamp. Unaware of what was about to happen to it, my left nipple cheerfully rose to the occasion and I couldn't help moaning in a combination of pleasure and pain. Seth attached the second clamp and tightened it before smiling at me.

"How's that?"

"Painful," I retorted.

He tugged on the silver chain that dangled between my breasts and I moaned as it pulled on my aching nipples. "Oh God! Don't – don't do that."

"Behave and I won't have to," he said.

He turned to Theo and said, "Is she wet enough to be fucked?"

God, why did his crudeness turn me on so much? And would there always be a small part of me that believed I was sick for wanting to be treated this way?

Theo was still holding my arms behind my back. He glanced at Seth and a silent communication rippled between them. Theo pressed a kiss against my cheek before saying, "Safe word, love?"

"Red," I said.

"We'll only stop for your safe word. Nothing else," Theo said.

"I know," I said in confusion. Why was he reminding me of that?

"Is she wet enough?" Seth repeated.

Theo cupped my pussy and rubbed it roughly. "Fuck, yes. She's dripping."

"Good. Are you ready to be fucked, Libby, or have you changed your mind?" Seth asked.

I gave him a blank look. Why the hell would he think I'd changed my mind? I was practically begging them to fuck me earlier before dinner, and...

My eyes widened. Holy shit, Seth and Theo were trying to give me exactly what I wanted. Fresh excitement raced through my veins and I was suddenly so turned on, I could hardly stand it. I had never taken a single acting class, had never joined the drama club or participated in a school play but I was about to play the part in my fantasy as eagerly as a waitress trying to make it in Hollywood.

I took a deep breath and said, "I've changed my mind."

Seth arched his eyebrow at me. "What did you say?"

"I've changed my mind. I – I don't want to fuck you. I'd like to go home now, please."

"Did you hear what she said, Theo?"

"I did."

A shiver of fear and anticipation went down my spine. Theo's voice had both deepened and roughened and he sounded angry. More fear licked along my veins but beneath it was – oh god, was it anticipation?

Seth reached out and traced my bottom lip with his finger. I tried to pull back from his touch and liquid dripped out of my pussy when Theo tightened his hold on my arms. I was trapped between them and that odd but compelling combination of fear and need tingled through me again.

"We gave you what you wanted tonight. Didn't we, Libby?"

"I- I don't know," I stammered.

"You don't know?" Seth's voice was silky soft. "I spanked you and Theo gave you an orgasm. Hell, I even made you dinner. Is that right?"

"Yes," I whispered.

"We did all of that for *you*, and now you're going to leave without spreading your pretty thighs and giving us a go at your cunt? Does that seem fair?"

"I don't have to – to have sex with you just because you did those things." I tried to sound strong but there was a waver in my voice that made

Seth smile.

"No, sweetheart, you don't. But do you know what they call girls like you?"

I shook my head and then moaned when Seth brushed his mouth across mine before whispering, "Cock tease."

I gasped in a combination of shock and pain when Theo tugged on the chain connecting the nipple clamps. It made my nipples throb and I whimpered when Seth leaned down and licked the swollen and tender tip of my right one. It sent pleasure straight to my pussy and I squeezed my thighs together in an attempt to ease the ache as Theo whispered in my ear.

"Are you a cock tease, Libby?"

"No," I moaned.

"Wrong answer," Theo replied before tugging again on the chain.

It sent fresh sparks of pleasure and pain radiating through me and I arched my back and stood on my tiptoes. Fuck, I was so wet I was about to drip all over the floor of the bedroom.

"Please," I cried out as Theo bit my neck and Seth nipped at my collarbone.

"Tell us what you are, Libby," Seth demanded.

"I – I'm a cock tease!" I said as Theo used his knee to push my thighs apart. He stuck his leg between mine and I rubbed against his denim-clad thigh with shameless need. "Oh, please!"

"Say it again," Seth demanded.

"I'm a cock tease," I said.

"That's right, you are. Your little cunt belongs to both of us and we'll fuck it whenever we want.

I barely heard Seth, I was rubbing my clit against Theo's hard thigh and I was so damn close to coming. I needed a little more friction, a little more pressure and…

I howled with pain when Seth pulled hard on the chain between my breasts. It yanked me back from the exquisite edge of my orgasm and I made inarticulate pleading noises as Theo pulled his leg from between mine.

"Fuck, Seth, I can't wait another goddamn minute."

Theo's voice was as ragged as my breath and to be honest, Seth was looking like he was on the verge of losing his control as well.

"Please, Seth, oh, please," I moaned.

He hesitated and then cursed under his breath before grabbing my arm and roughly pulling me to the bed. "On your hands and knees, facing the headboard, Libby."

I obeyed him without hesitation. Part of me was sorry I had ruined my fantasy so quickly, but I felt nearly wild. If they didn't give me what I wanted, what I *needed*, I would lose my goddamn mind.

I clambered onto the bed and dropped to my hands and knees, staring at the headboard. Seth and Theo were tearing off their clothes in record time and I only made a small whimper of protest when Seth wrapped a heavy chain around the center iron spindle of the headboard and grabbed both my wrists.

"Hands up," he demanded hoarsely.

I lifted my hands, balancing myself on my knees as Seth threaded the chain through the hoops in the leather cuffs around my wrists before securing the chain to the headboard.

I squealed in surprise when Theo grabbed my hips and lifted me up enough for Seth to slide beneath me. My legs were spread wide around his hips and my back was arched from the way my hands were tied. Seth was already wearing a condom and I resisted when his hands replaced Theo's on my hips and pulled.

"Libby," he said warningly, "lower your tight pussy on my dick, right now."

"Seth," I whispered. Even as turned on as I was, my insecurities were rearing their ugly head. "Seth, don't make me do this."

"You're going to ride me, sweetheart, because if you don't, I'll tell Theo to pull that plug from your ass and replace it with his cock. What do you think, Libby? You think your ass is stretched enough to take Theo's cock?"

I stared at Seth and knew he meant every word of what he was saying. I must have hesitated too long because he pulled hard on the chain between my breasts. I cried out and quickly lowered my body until the tip of his cock brushed against my pussy. He groaned and reached between us, guiding his cock to my entrance. I pushed down and we both moaned when he entered me fully with one hard thrust.

Thanks to my hands being restrained, I had to bend over him, leaving my breasts in his face. He took advantage of it, sucking on my protruding nipples and pulling on the clamps with his teeth. I moaned and pleaded for mercy as the bed dipped and Theo kneeled between Seth's legs behind me.

I was stuffed full of Seth's cock, restrained with my nipples clamped and there was so much lust coursing through my veins, I was afraid my heart would explode from it. The deep breath I took that was meant to help calm me, turned into a wailing scream of pure pleasure. Theo was pushing and tugging on the plug in my ass while his fingers pinched my clit and that was it for me. I came with another hard scream as the pleasure rolled through me in endless tumbling waves that made my entire body shake. Dimly, I was aware of Seth thrusting into me from below, of the way his hard cock pounded into my pussy. He made a harsh roar that shook me to my core with its intensity and arched upward. There was a brief flash of pain as he thrust deep and then it was his turn to shake and moan.

"Seth, fucking move!" Theo's voice was the sound of a desperate animal.

I cried out when he yanked on my hips, pulling my body up until Seth's cock popped out of me.

"Goddammit move, Seth!" Theo said furiously.

With a low groan Seth slid out from under me, rolling to the far side of the bed and laying on his back as he gasped for air.

My thighs were pulled apart so wide that the muscles screamed in protest. I hung my head and took great gasping breaths of air and then squealed with pleasure when Theo pushed in to the hilt.

"Fuck, oh fuck," he chanted in a low moan as he pushed and retreated with hard and punishing strokes. I braced my hands against the headboard, the chain that bound me to it rattling loudly as new tingles of exquisite pleasure started up in my pussy.

"Oh God, no," I moaned. "I can't have another one. I can't have... oh God!"

Without breaking his rhythm, Theo had reached under me and was rubbing at my clit. It was too much and I tried to break free, crying out when his hand wrapped in my hair and yanked my head back.

"No," he snarled into my ear. "You come for me right now, baby. Come all over my cock with your tight pussy!"

He pulled on my clit and I screamed as I climaxed again. This one was just as intense as the first one and I shook wildly as white light exploded behind my eyelids. Theo shouted my name before driving me down into the mattress. His big body shook on top of mine and his hand pulled hard at my hair as he came deep inside of me.

His weight was making it hard to breathe and I protested my lack of oxygen. He pulled out and collapsed on the other side of me, nearly falling off the bed in the process. I pulled at the chain connecting me to the bed and Seth quickly unclasped it before tossing the chain on the floor beside the bed. He rolled me over onto my back and I stared glassy-eyed at him as he made soft crooning noises into my ear and rubbed my quivering belly and thighs.

"Such a good girl, Libby," he said. "She's our good girl, isn't she, Theo?"

"Yes," Theo said. He was removing his condom and he tossed it into the trash can next to the bed. He rolled to his side to face us and propped his head up with one trembling hand.

"Fuck, that was unbelievable."

I stared mutely at them and Seth smoothed the hair away from my sweaty face. "You okay, Libs?"

"Yes," I whispered. "I'm sorry."

"Sorry for what?" Theo gave me a puzzled look.

"For – for ruining the fantasy," I said. "I tried to pretend I didn't want it for longer but..."

I trailed off and blushed when both Seth and Theo laughed.

"Baby, it was amazing. Besides, this was all for you so if you wanted to end the role playing five minutes in, that's perfectly fine."

"I really liked it," I whispered.

"Good," Seth said. "We liked it too and we can always try it again and see if we can make it past five minutes."

I didn't reply. What had happened was so intense, I couldn't imagine trying it again any time soon. I needed time to recuperate, time to reflect on what it was about me that found this type of role playing so appealing. This was my only chance to live out that fantasy and I had kind of ruined it, but I refused to feel bad about it. I couldn't feel bad about it. Even if it was short-lived, it was fucking amazing and I would masturbate to this night in my head for years to come. I was sure of it.

"Are you ready, sweetheart?" Seth asked.

"Ready for what?" I gave him a look of confusion. Oh God, they didn't want another round already did they? My legs were like noodles and my heart was still beating like a runaway freight train. I needed some recovery time.

"This is going to hurt," Theo said.

"What's going to hurt?" I asked as he released the clamp around my right nipple and Seth released the clamp on my left. For a moment there was nothing and I shifted on the bed. "It doesn't hurt. It doesn't even...oh fucking hell!"

The blood was returning to my swollen nipples and oh sweet Jesus, did it fucking hurt! Tears gushed from my eyes and I tried to clap my hands over my nipples in some misguided attempt to soothe them. Before I could touch them, both Theo and Seth took a nipple into their mouth. They soothed and licked my nipples with their warm mouths and tongues. It helped ease the pain and tingling and I moaned and bit my bottom lip as they lifted their heads.

"Sorry, sweetheart," Seth said. He wiped the moisture from my cheeks as Theo rubbed the soft skin between my breasts.

"Fuck, that hurts," I said.

"I know and we're sorry," Theo said.

"Are you?" I squinted at them in suspicion and Theo laughed before rolling me to my side. He pulled the plug from my ass and tossed it into a basket on the nightstand.

"Should I go now?" I mumbled. I didn't want to go. I was tired and warm and wanted to sleep but spending the night had never been part of the deal despite sleeping over last night

Theo curled up behind me and stroked my side and hip as Seth rubbed my upper chest. He avoided touching my nipples and I relaxed into Theo's embrace as Seth kissed my forehead.

"No, sweetheart. You're spending the night with us."

"K, cool," I mumbled again before yawning. "Night, guys."

"Goodnight, love," Theo whispered into my ear.

Chapter Eight

I stared at the whiteboard in my office before adding another note to myself at the bottom. My cell phone rang and I snagged it from where I'd tossed it on my desk. It was Thursday afternoon and I had spent most of the day in my office finishing up a file. It was the last file on my desk and if I didn't find something else, Friday and Monday morning were going to be ridiculously long. I glanced at my phone screen and smiled. The number was very familiar and I hit the answer button.

"Good afternoon, Elizabeth speaking."

"Libby!" Charles Emerson's southern drawl washed over me. "It's Charles Emerson. How the fuck are you?"

I ignored my urge to laugh. Charles was a second-generation oil driller. He was a big, tough Texan with permanently stained hands, a handlebar mustache that would make Sam Elliot jealous and a big booming voice. He bred horses in his spare time, cursed like a sailor and went to church without fail every Sunday. He also had a wife he very obviously adored and four children who were all involved in the family business.

His company, Etco Drilling Ltd., was my previous firm's biggest client. I was assigned to the Etco file in my first year. I had a feeling that my old boss - a sexist pig of a man who only hired female lawyers because he was forced to - believed that Charles with his quick temper and hard and grizzled exterior would eat me alive. Instead, we had forged an unlikely friendship over the next eight years. When I told Charles that I was thinking of leaving my firm and pursuing a partnership opportunity, he hadn't hesitated to let me know he would follow me. I wasn't naïve or stupid enough to think that having a multi-million-dollar drilling company as a loyal client wasn't part of the reason that I got the partnership at Martin, Clarke and Bones.

"Hello, Charles. I'm good. How are you?" I said.

"Can't complain. Well I could, but ain't no one around who cares enough to listen."

There was an outraged voice in the background and Charles gave a big booming laugh. "Now I'm in trouble with my Mags. She says hello and wants you to check your mailbox. She sent your Christmas present to your new address last week."

I felt a rush of love for Charles' wife Maggie. "She did? That's so sweet. Please tell her I said thank you and ask her if she found that knitting pattern she was looking for online."

He harrumphed irritably as his short temper got

the best of him. "Jesus Christ, I ain't no messenger boy, Elizabeth. Call her up once the holidays are over and ask her yourself. She's been pining for a good chinwag with ya anyway."

I laughed. "All right, I will. Now, what can I help you with?"

"Nothing work related," Charles said. His voice softened a touch. "Just wanted to check in on ya, make sure the new job is going okay and to say Merry Christmas and shit like that."

Out of the corner of my eye I saw Sandra stick her head into my office. I waved her in as I shifted my cell phone to my other ear. "It's going well."

"Good," he said. "Real fuckin' glad to hear it, Libby. You have a good Christmas, okay?"

"You too. Give my love to Maggie and tell her I'll call her in the new year."

"Will do."

Like always, he hung up without saying goodbye and I grinned at Sandra as I hit the end button on my cell phone. "Sorry, Sandra. That was Charles from Etco Drilling."

"I spoke to him this morning. He called the office while you were meeting with Mario and got a little huffy when I wouldn't interrupt you," Sandra said.

I laughed. "That sounds like Charles."

"I was actually just coming in to talk to you about Etco," Sandra said.

"All right." I walked back to my desk and sat down in my chair. I thought I did a good job of hiding my flinch, but Sandra frowned at me immediately.

"Are you hurt, Libby? This is the second time I've seen you wince when you sat down."

Shit.

"Uh, no. I did a bit too much yoga this week and strained some muscles," I lied.

Truthfully, my ass was covered in big purple bruises and it hurt like fire when I sat. Not to mention how painful my damn nipples were. Despite the pain, I didn't feel any regret for what I'd done. In fact, I was almost late for work because I kept admiring the way my bruised ass looked in the mirror. There was a bruise in the shape of a handprint on my lower left cheek. I had stared at it for over a minute, knowing that if Seth put his hand over the bruise it would be the perfect match. That thought had made me shiver with lust and even now, I could feel fresh lust trickling through me.

"Right," Sandra said.

Shit. A topic change was sorely needed. "So, what is your question about Etco?"

"No questions. Emmett asked me to mention to you that Seth and Theo aren't going to be available to help you with the file until after Christmas," Sandra said.

"Oh really?" I tried to sound casual.

"Yes. We have a high-maintenance client in Georgia and," Sandra paused and rolled her eyes, "they've had another self-proclaimed crisis and insisted that Seth and Theo fly out this afternoon."

Dismay rippled through me and Sandra gave me an odd look. "Libby? Are you okay? Is there a problem with the Etco file?"

"No, everything's fine." I made myself smile cheerfully at her. "When are they back. Do you know?"

"I booked their return flight for late Monday morning. The client wanted me to book them to come back on Wednesday. Can you believe it? Tuesday is Christmas for heaven's sake!" Sandra rolled her eyes again. "I know Jeff and Mario have been urging Emmett to drop them as clients and I think this might be the straw that breaks the camel's back. Anyway, they're coming back Monday morning, but Jeff already told them not to come into the office and to start their Christmas holidays with their families."

"Well, I'm sure it will be fine for the Etco file," I said.

"Good," Sandra said. "Are you leaving tomorrow or Saturday?"

I gave her a blank look and she frowned at me. "Aren't you driving home this weekend for Christmas?"

I shook my head. "No, I'm staying here. It's such a long drive, you know?"

"I guess," Sandra said slowly. "What are you doing for Christmas?"

"Oh, I, uh, I'm, um…"

"You're not spending Christmas alone?" Sandra asked in horror.

"I am," I admitted.

"You can come to my house," Sandra said. "We're eating dinner at two."

"No, thank you," I said. "I'm not intruding on your family dinner and besides, I'm looking forward to having Christmas by myself this year."

It wasn't entirely true, but I couldn't tell a woman I barely knew that I was looking forward to not spending Christmas with my overbearing and disapproving mother.

"Libby, no one should spend Christmas alone," Sandra said.

I shrugged. "Honestly, I need to be alone this year, Sandra."

Sandra gave me a searching look before sighing. "Okay, well if you change your mind, it's an open invitation. I'll email you my address. Come over at any time."

"Thanks, Sandra. That's very nice of you and I appreciate it," I said.

"Well, I mean it," she replied.

"I know," I said and then to mollify her, I said, "I'll think about it, okay?"

"Okay," she said. "Are you coming in Monday morning?"

"I was going to," I replied.

"Don't bother," she said. "No one is coming in. It's going to be dead in here and most of our clients are used to us having limited staff during the holiday break. I know the other partners told you not to come in. Take their advice and stay home and sleep in."

I laughed. "All right. I won't come in on Monday."

"Good," Sandra said with a satisfied smile.

જે જ

Monday afternoon, I stepped out the shower and

wrapped the towel around my wet body. I wiped the steam from the mirror and stared at my reflection before running a comb through my hair. There was a small pink box on the bathroom vanity and I flipped the lid off, staring at the butt plug sitting inside of it.

I'd purchased it Thursday night, walking into the adult store with a vague sense of embarrassment. I'd never been in a store like that before and I'd walked the entire store staring at the inventory with equal amounts of curiosity and shock. I'd purchased a butt plug and lube, a small part of me wondering what the store employee was thinking as she placed it in the pink box. Once I was home, I'd inserted the plug and worn it the entire evening as I ate my dinner of cold cereal, and used my laptop to watch a couple of shows on Hulu.

Now, I sighed and put the lid back on the box. I'd already worn it for a few hours this morning. I'd worn it for a few hours each day on the weekend as well. Although why I bothered, I didn't know. I hadn't heard a single word from Seth or Theo since I'd left their bed Thursday morning.

As I'd been doing all weekend, I tried to console myself. They were working, we weren't dating – hell, we weren't even friends – so why would they contact me? It didn't hurt my feelings that they hadn't texted me even once. Why would they?

Why are you still wearing that damn plug? Inner me whispered.

"Once the holidays are over, I'm sure we'll pick up where we left off. I still haven't had sex with both of them at once." I said to my reflection.

Are you sure about that? They haven't contacted you once since they left. Yeah, you're not dating them, but wouldn't it be at least polite of them to send you one text?

Fuck, inner me just didn't know when to shut the hell up.

Maybe they're tired of you. You told them what Wayne said to you – maybe they realized they don't want to be those men with the fat girlfriend either. Maybe they –

Shut up! I snarled at my inner self. *Just shut up! We're not dating and I don't care if they don't call or text me. I want one thing from them and that's it, so shut the fuck up for once!*

Mercifully, my inner self lapsed into silence. I rubbed at my forehead before leaving the bathroom and walking to my bedroom. I dressed in yoga pants and a t-shirt, not bothering with a bra or underwear, and stared at my pathetic air mattress for a moment.

I was lying to myself and didn't want to admit it. I missed Theo and Seth. More than I should have if I was only using them for sex. I sighed and stared out the window at the falling snow. The last four days had passed agonizingly slow and I was already going a little stir crazy. I missed my stuff, I missed my friends and there was a part of me that wanted to jump in my car and drive home. If I left now, I could be home before midnight. Mom would be happy to have me home. Then, at least, I wouldn't spend the next week roaming a nearly empty apartment, eating cold cereal and wishing I was doing something inappropriate like fucking my funny, sweet and stupidly hot coworkers.

I could tell myself repeatedly that it wasn't over and that we would simply pick up where we left off when the craziness of the holidays was over, but not hearing from them had rattled me badly. Thinking they would text or call just to say hello was ridiculous so why was I hurt that they hadn't?

I needed to stop thinking about them, needed to stop wondering if they would –

My cell phone rang and I snatched it up from the floor next to the air mattress. It was my mother. For the first time in forever, I was eager to talk to her. It would take my mind off Theo and Seth and maybe I would let her talk me into driving home. I hit the answer button as I walked to the kitchen.

"Hey, Mom!" I said cheerfully. "How are you?"

There was a pause and then my mother said suspiciously, "Libby? Why are you so happy?"

"Why shouldn't I be?" I asked.

She snorted. "Maybe because you've left your mother all alone at Christmas? Do you even feel bad at all, Elizabeth?"

Guilt flooded through me immediately. "Mom, of course I do. I was even thinking that maybe I would - "

"I don't think you do, Libby." My mother steamrolled right over me. "I think you're doing this as some kind of punishment, because I was honest about my disappointment over the way you treated Wayne."

"The way I treated Wayne?" I could hear the irritation in my voice and I tried to rein it in. It was

Christmas and I didn't want to fight with my mother, no matter how difficult our relationship was. "Mom, Wayne cheated on me."

"Oh for God's sake, Elizabeth," my mother retorted, "when are you going to let that go?"

My jaw dropped. "Let that go? You're kidding me, right?"

"Libby, honey, I think you need to give Wayne another chance. You refuse to lose the weight and because of that, he's as good as you're going to get. Men are visual creatures, they don't want a fat girl."

My stomach clenched and I said, "Do you hear yourself, Mom? You just called your own kid fat. Does that seem like something a mother would do?"

"If she's a mother who has her child's best interest at heart, then yes."

Anger flooded through me and I welcomed it. Embraced it and let it flourish. "No, Mom. That's isn't true and I won't let you keep treating me this way."

My doorbell rang and I stalked to the front door and yanked it open without even bothering to look at who it was.

"Treating you what way?" My mother said with that tone of fake hurt that made my skin crawl. "I love you, Libby and I only want what's best for you."

I barely heard her. I was staring wide-eyed at Theo and Seth standing on my doorstep. Without saying anything, I stepped aside so they could brush past me. "Mom, I have to go."

"Of course you do," my mother snapped. "You always have to go."

"I'll call you tomorrow," I said and ended the call as Seth closed the door.

The three of us stood silently in the front hall before I stuttered, "W-what are you doing here?"

"What are you doing here?" Seth countered. "We thought you would be driving home to your family for Christmas."

I shrugged. "I'm not. If you thought I was gone, why did you stop by?"

"We stopped at the office after our flight landed," Theo said. "We overheard Sandra telling Allison that you would be alone at Christmas. Why aren't you going home?"

"It's a long story but let's just say that it's preferable to spending Christmas with my mother," I said.

There was another moment of awkward silence and I shifted from foot to foot before saying, "Well, thanks for stopping by. Merry Christmas."

Seth scowled at me. "You're not spending Christmas alone, Libby. You're spending it with us."

I blinked at him. "I'm not spending Christmas with yours or Theo's family. I don't even know them and how would you even explain who I was? Oh hey, fam, this is my pathetic boss who doesn't have anywhere to go for Christmas."

"Theo's parents are in Europe for Christmas and mine are in Montana at my grandparents," Seth replied. "It's just the two of us for Christmas this year."

I ignored the excitement brewing in my belly. "Oh, well, I appreciate the offer but I'm looking forward to my alone time."

Theo rolled his eyes. "Eating cold cereal and sleeping on an air mattress?"

"I don't need your pity invite to spend Christmas with you!" I suddenly hissed at them.

"It's not a pity invite," Theo replied.

"Yeah, right," I muttered.

Seth gave me a thoughtful look. "We're sorry we didn't call you while we were in Georgia, Libby. We didn't mean to upset you."

I was surprised by his intuitiveness to my emotional reaction. I chewed at my bottom lip before saying, "Why would you? I didn't expect you to call me and I'm not upset that you didn't."

Seth glanced at Theo. "Do you think she's lying to us because she wants a spanking or because she thinks we want to hear that she isn't upset."

I backed away, my hands dropping to cover my ass automatically. "I'm not lying."

Seth grinned and stepped toward me before hauling me into his embrace. He nuzzled my neck and pressed a kiss against my cheek. "You are lying and you should be upset with us. We were dicks not to text or call but we were busy with an absolute bastard of a client and," he paused and glanced at Theo.

"We weren't sure if you wanted us to contact you," Theo finished. "All we have is your work cell phone number and…"

He trailed off and I found myself feeling grateful for their discretion. Work phones were the property of the office and any texts could be monitored. I didn't want anyone at work knowing what I was doing with them and they were trying to respect that.

"I'm sorry. I'm being a total bitch and I had no right to be upset that I didn't hear from you. I just missed you both," I admitted.

"We're glad you're upset," Seth said and winced when Theo punched him in the arm. "That didn't come out right. What I mean is that we're glad you missed us because holy fuck, did we miss you."

He squeezed my ass and I smiled at him even though a pang of disappointment went through me. It was fine that they had missed me because of the sex. I didn't want more from them.

Seth stepped away and Theo took his place. He cupped my breast and circled my hardening nipple with his thumb. "Pack a bag and come spend Christmas with us, Libby. Please."

"I – okay," I whispered.

"Good," Theo said. He pressed a kiss against my mouth. "Come on, love. I'll help you pack."

&

"What's this?" I stared at the wrapped package that Seth placed in my lap. It was later that evening. After arriving at their home, I'd helped Seth cook dinner and the three of us had enjoyed the meal with a couple glasses of wine. I thought we'd go to the bedroom and have sex but instead, they'd led me into the living room. The lights in the tree gleamed as Theo turned on the TV. Explaining it was a Christmas Eve tradition, we had watched two movies – *Elf* and *A Christmas Story* – both men laughing like little kids and quoting lines as we watched.

"It's a gift for you," Seth said.

"I didn't get you guys anything," I replied.

"You weren't supposed to," Theo said. "Open it, love."

I ripped off the packaging and opened the lid of the box. Nestled in pink tissue paper was a heart-shaped jewelled anal plug. I stared at it for a moment before bursting into giggles.

"Do you like it, sweetheart?" Seth asked with a grin.

"It's the most unique Christmas gift I've ever gotten," I laughed.

"And most romantic, right?" Theo said.

I laughed even harder. "Oh, definitely."

"Theo wanted to go with the kitty cat tail one, but I talked him out of it," Seth said.

I poked Theo in the stomach. "Don't be a brat."

"What do you say we go to the bedroom and try out your new Christmas gift?" Theo said before kissing me. "If we use it for a few more days, you should be stretched enough."

"I've, uh, been using a butt plug every day since Thursday," I said. My cheeks reddened and I wished I didn't feel embarrassed by my admission.

Seth gave me a look of glee. "Seriously?"

"Yes," I said. "I bought one and have been using it daily."

"Fuck, you are the perfect fucking woman," Seth said before leaning in and kissing me hard on the mouth. "Theo, get our perfect woman to the bedroom right now while I shut off the lights.

Theo tossed the box with the plug on the couch and pulled me to my feet. I followed him to the bedroom and he undressed me and himself in record time before pushing me onto my back on the bed.

"Theo, what – oh my god!"

Theo was lying between my legs with his face buried in my pussy before I could even blink. "Theo!" I moaned when he sucked on my clit.

He raised his head. "Yes, love?"

"Wh-what are you doing?"

"It's called foreplay," he said with a teasing grin.

"Shouldn't we wait for Seth?" I whispered. My hands were already tangling in his hair and I whimpered with pleasure when Theo nipped my inner thigh.

"He'll be here soon. I've spent the last four days dreaming about your cunt and how sweet it tastes. Don't even think of denying me, Libby."

"I'm not," I said quickly.

"Good. Let's see how wet I can make your pussy before Seth shows up." He dove back into my pussy and I closed my eyes and arched my back when he licked my clit with warm strokes of his tongue. He teased and licked and nipped until I was digging my feet into the small of his back and grinding my pussy against his mouth.

My eyes popped open the moment I felt a warm mouth cover my aching nipple. Seth was lying on the bed beside me and he licked and sucked at my nipple almost lazily as Theo ate my pussy with undisguised enthusiasm.

"Are your nipples still sore, sweetheart?" Seth

asked.

"No," I panted as I rocked my hips against Theo's face. "No, they – they're fine."

"I'm glad. If you're our good girl, we won't use the clamps tonight."

I didn't reply and Seth gave my nipple a hard pinch. "Libby? Are you paying attention to me?"

"Fuck, no I'm not paying attention to you!" I retorted. I glared at him and he laughed and pinched my other nipple until I cried out.

"Theo, stop for a minute," Seth said.

"No! Theo, do not stop!" I shouted.

Theo lifted his head and smiled at Seth. "What's up?"

"Goddammit!" I shouted and tried to shove Theo's head back between my thighs.

Seth grabbed my wrists and yanked them above my head, pinning them to the bed. I cried out when Theo gave my pussy two hard slaps. It stung like hell so why was I spreading my legs in a silent plea for more?

Instead of slapping me, Theo pressed a kiss against the swollen lips of my pussy as Seth nipped my collarbone. "Be our good girl, Libby."

"I am, Sir" I said desperately.

"Say it."

"I'll be your good girl, Sir," I said frantically.

"What do good girls do?"

I stared at him for a moment before hit with inspiration. "They suck cock, Sir."

Seth smiled and I felt an absurd tingle of pride when he said, "That's right. Open up, good girl."

I opened my mouth as Seth shifted until he was

kneeling next to me. He slipped a hand under my neck and lifted my head, supporting me as I sucked his cock into my mouth.

"Fuck, that's good," he muttered as he thrust in and out of my mouth. "Suck my cock like my good girl."

Theo sucked on my clit again and I moaned around Seth's cock. The vibration made Seth groan and he thrust even harder into my mouth. I barely noticed my inability to breathe or the spit that was running down my chin as Seth pushed in and out. Theo was teasing my clit with small flicks of his tongue and I was on the verge of climaxing.

Theo nipped my clit and I screamed, the sound muffled by Seth's thick cock, as I came in a violent rush of dizzying pleasure. Theo held my lower body still with hard hands on my hips and licked and sucked at my clit as my climax rolled through me.

I screamed again and Seth's hand tightened around my neck before he abruptly pulled out. I sucked in a lungful of air and let it out in a loud moan as Theo rubbed my oversensitive clit with the pad of his thumb. I jerked away and waited for the spank, but Theo simply pressed a kiss against my quivering thigh before standing up and opening the nightstand drawer. He pulled out a bottle of lube and condoms and handed a condom and the lube to Seth. Both men rolled on their condoms as I panted and moaned and twitched on the bed.

The bed dipped as Theo reclined on his back. "Climb on, Libby."

My legs were still shaking but I sat up and

straddled him. I realized I wasn't worrying one bit about hurting him and scored myself a mental victory as Theo cupped both my breasts. "You're so beautiful, Libby."

"Thank you," I whispered. "So are you. Both of you."

Theo cupped my face and tenderly stroked my cheekbone with his thumb. "If it hurts too much or you want to stop at any time, say your safe word, okay? We won't be upset."

I glanced at Seth who was opening the bottle of lube. He smiled and leaned forward to kiss me. "We won't be, sweetheart. I promise."

"Okay," I said. "So, uh what do we do first?"

"First you put my cock in that soaking wet cunt of yours," Theo said.

I blushed a little but grasped Theo's cock at the base and guided it to my opening. He was right about being soaking wet and I sank down on his cock with ease despite his size. Theo released his breath in a low groan before urging me to lean over him.

I braced my hands on the bed on either side of his head and we kissed with slow, deep strokes of our tongues as Seth kneeled between Theo's spread legs. Theo made a few lazy thrusts into my pussy as we kissed and I moaned into his mouth. God, it felt so good to have his cock again.

Feeling a little drunk on pleasure, I whispered, "I love your cock, Theo."

He nuzzled my neck before sucking on my earlobe. "I love your hot little pussy, Libby. You're an amazing woman and fucking you is all I can think about."

I moaned when he cupped my breasts and tugged on my nipples. Behind me, Seth was rubbing lube into my anus and I took a deep breath and pushed against his fingers when he pushed them deep into my ass. He made a scissoring motion with his fingers to stretch me. I pushed my breast against Theo's mouth and he sucked obligingly on my nipple as he made gentle little thrusts with his hips.

"Are you ready, sweetheart?" Seth asked.

"Yes."

"I'll go slow, I promise. Remember to breathe and to push back against me, okay?"

I looked over my shoulder at him. "Yes."

"You're sure?"

"Positive. Fuck my ass, Seth," I said.

He groaned and a look of almost feral need crossed his face before he moved a little closer. "Theo, stop moving."

Theo held still and gave me a reassuring look as Seth pressed the head of his dick against my anus. I took a deep breath and pushed back against the steady pressure. I groaned and bit at my lip. Fuck, even with the plugs, it was hurting more than I thought it would.

I was about to say stop and ask for more time when Theo's hand slipped between my legs and rubbed at my swollen clit.

"Oh!" I squeaked as pleasure immediately mixed with the pain. "Oh, that helps!"

"Good," Theo said. "Concentrate on my fingers touching you, love. Your little clit is so swollen and hard. You want to come again, don't you?"

"Yes," I moaned. "I really do."

"Soon," Theo said soothingly.

There was a sudden flare of pain and I groaned. Seth rubbed my ass and Theo rubbed my clit as I hung my head and took deep breaths. The pain subsided rather quickly, leaving a feeling of dull pressure that was actually a little pleasurable.

"Is it in?" I panted.

"The head is," Seth replied.

I groaned and swivelled my head to stare at him. "Just the head?"

I already felt stuffed to the brim and couldn't imagine taking any more of Seth's cock. "I don't think I can take any more."

"Yes, you can," Seth said. "Take my cock up your ass like a good girl or I'll give you a spanking."

That made me clench around both men's dicks and Theo groaned. "Jesus, Seth, stop threatening to spank her!"

"Rub her clit again," Seth ordered.

Theo rubbed my clit and I moaned and rubbed my pussy against his fingers as Seth pushed and retreated slowly until I felt his pelvis pressing against my ass and he made a satisfied grunt.

"Good girl," he said.

"Oh God," I moaned. "It's too much. I can't take it."

Seth ignored me and made a few gentle thrusts that sent lightning coursing up and down my nerve endings.

"Fuck!" I squealed. "Oh God, that's – that's

good."

Both men laughed and I blushed but gave Theo a pleading look. "Please touch my clit again."

He shook his head. "No, we're going to make you come with just our dicks this time, love."

I gave him another pleading look, but he ignored it and cupped my breasts as Seth held my hips. They began a slow rhythm of one man pushing in while the other withdrew. It made my toes curl and I panted and moaned as they both fucked me.

"Feel good, little Libby?" Seth pressed on my lower back.

"Oh God, fuck, yes," I groaned. "I think – harder, please."

They moved faster and harder. My body was buzzing and twitching with pleasure and I wasn't sure if I should be happy or ashamed at how much pleasure I was deriving from a dick in my ass. Having Seth's cock in my ass made Theo's cock feel even thicker in my pussy. I squeezed around both of them experimentally and both men immediately did hard and out-of-control thrusts that made me squeal.

"Fuck! Don't squeeze like that, love," Theo begged below me as Seth panted harshly behind me.

I squeezed again and Seth slapped my ass hard. I squealed a second time and turned my head to pout at him.

"Behave," he said but there was a pleading tone to it that I'd never heard in his voice before.

I grinned and rocked my body a little. "What's wrong, Seth? Going to blow your load before you make me come?"

I received another glorious slap to the ass for my impertinence. I flushed with happiness and didn't object when both men pounded roughly into me. In fact, their roughness ratcheted up my excitement and I clutched at Theo's shoulders and made soft cries for more.

"She's so fucking tight," Theo suddenly moaned. "Seth, I can't…"

"Make her come first," Seth demanded but he sounded as frantic as Theo.

"Fuck, I'm trying," Theo panted.

To my surprise and delight, he reached beneath me and rubbed my clit in hard, rough circles. I cried out happily and rocked against his fingers. I was coming against his fingers in less than thirty seconds, my pussy and ass tightening around their cocks helplessly as I climaxed. Seth made a hoarse roar of need and then both men were pounding into me. I clung to Theo as a new and unrecognizable pleasure grew in my body.

"Oh, oh, God," I moaned. "What is that? What – oh fuck!" I was gasping and sobbing with need as both men moved harder and faster. I couldn't stop clenching around both dicks. The motion heightened my pleasure and I heard Theo groan loudly.

He arched beneath me. I barely registered that he was coming as Seth shoved his dick in and out of my ass. The only thing mattered was the orgasm that was agonizingly close. I squeezed my eyes shut and ground my pussy against Theo's dick as I reached for my climax. As Seth made a low roar and his hands dug into my hips, I shrieked with pleasure and came wildly. My body shook and I screamed again before collapsing on top of Theo.

I could feel Theo's heart beating like a drum beneath my cheek and I told myself to roll off of him before I crushed him. I made a half-hearted attempt to move before collapsing on him again. He rubbed my back and I was only vaguely aware of Seth moving away to the other side of the bed.

After a few minutes, Theo kissed the top of my head. "Okay?" He asked hoarsely.

"Yes," I mumbled. "Sorry, I'll move."

"You're fine," he said as his arms tightened around my waist. "Give it a minute."

I snuggled against him and it wasn't until his heart was beating a normal rhythm again that I eased off of him and lay weakly between the two men.

Seth had already removed his condom and as Theo removed his and tossed it in the trash, I stared at Seth. He was lying on his back, staring at the ceiling and I touched his chest tentatively.

"Seth? Was it okay for you?"

"Okay?" He rasped. "Libby, I nearly fucking passed out when I came."

I laughed and leaned against Theo when he spooned me and kissed the back of my shoulder. I squeezed his hand. "Theo? You, um, enjoyed it, right?"

"Do you really have to ask?" He said before patting my ass. "How are you? Are you sore? Do you want me to run you a hot bath?"

"I'm good," I said. I wasn't lying. My ass was

a little sore, but the rest of my body felt incredible. I'd never had orgasms like that before. Hell, the last one was so good, I thought my head was going to blow off.

"It was amazing," I said suddenly. "Thank you so much. It was incredible."

"Good, we're glad," Seth said.

"I don't think I'll be able to ever have sex with just one man again," I said without thinking.

There was silence and I cleared my throat. "Uh, I didn't mean – that is, I know this is it for us. I wasn't trying to imply that the two of you had to keep fucking me."

"What if we want to keep fucking you?" Theo asked.

I stiffened and Theo sighed. "Sorry, I shouldn't have said that."

I licked my lips. "Did you want to keep having sex with me?"

"No," Seth said bluntly and my sudden hope deflated like a balloon.

"I should go," I whispered. I didn't regret what I had done with them but the knowledge that they didn't want to continue hurt way more than it should have considering we had agreed on a casual sex agreement.

Before I could squirm away from them, Theo's arm was tightening around my waist and Seth was cupping my face. "Sweetheart, we don't want to just have sex with you. We want to see if it could be something more."

I stared in shock at him. "You – you're kidding, right?"

"No," Theo said solemnly. "We're not."

"We're good together, Libs," Seth said. "You know we are. I know it's not a conventional relationship, but you said yourself that you couldn't sleep with only one man anymore. You don't have to. You have two men right here very willing to kiss, lick, suck and spank this delicious little body of yours. Let us."

"I'm your boss," I said in a low voice. "If the other partners found out..."

"We can find new jobs," Theo said.

"Are you – you can't quit your job because we enjoy fucking each other," I said. "Have you lost your minds?"

Seth laughed. "No, I don't think so. Neither of us thought we'd be at Martin, Clarke and Bones forever anyway."

"You can't quit your job for me," I whispered. "We don't even know if this dating thing would work out."

"No, I suppose we don't," Seth said thoughtfully. "Tell you what, we'll give it a couple of months. We can keep it a secret from our coworkers if we're very careful. If we can convince you at the end of two months that this could be something more than just sex, we'll start looking for new jobs. What do you think?"

They waited patiently as I thought it over. What they were suggesting was madness, but it was incredibly tempting. I liked both of them, and getting to know them better was dangerously appealing.

"What if it doesn't work out between us?" I

asked.

"We won't say anything to the other partners about what happened between us if it doesn't," Theo assured me.

I blinked at him. That thought hadn't even crossed my mind. I knew instinctively that they wouldn't use a failed relationship to blackmail me, just like they weren't using what we were doing now to blackmail me. They were good men – possibly the best men I'd ever met - and I would be a fool not to see where this would lead.

"I only meant that it will be incredibly awkward at work," I said.

"Possibly," Seth agreed. "But that's only if it didn't work out. Do you believe that it won't?"

I studied him before shaking my head. "No, I don't think that."

Theo nuzzled my neck. "So, is that a yes to dating us?"

"This is crazy as hell but yes. Let's see where this goes," I replied.

A huge smile crossed Seth's face and he pressed a kiss against my mouth as Theo kissed my neck.

"You won't regret it, sweetheart. We promise."

END

About the Author

Ramona Gray is a Canadian romance author. She currently lives in Alberta with her awesome husband and her mutant Chihuahua. She's addicted to home improvement shows, good coffee, and reading and writing about the steamier moments in life.

If you would like more information about Ramona, please visit her at:

www.ramonagray.ca

Books by Ramona Gray

Individual Books

The Escort
Saving Jax
The Assistant
One Night
Sharing Del
Filthy Appeal

Other World Series

The Vampire's Kiss (Book One)
The Vampire's Love (Book Two)
The Shifter's Mate (Book Three)
Rescued By The Wolf (Book Four)
Claiming Quinn (Book Five)
Choosing Rose (Book Six)

Undeniable Series

Undeniably His
Undeniably Hers
Undeniably Theirs

Working Men Series

The Mechanic
The Carpenter
The Bartender
The Welder
The Electrician
The Landscaper